Saving Face

Saving Face

T.J. Dell

For my husband Daniel,
Your love and support are a constant in
my life that I rely on at all times.

Chapter One

It was probably too late to ring the bell. Alyssa Maddow stood outside on the sidewalk in front of her best friend, Brent Carter's, house. She pressed the glow button on her cell phone. 11:43—definitely too late to ring the bell. Ms. Carter worked at the post office and she usually worked early so she would most likely already be asleep. Brent might be asleep too, come to think of it. Making up her mind Alyssa continued down the sidewalk to the next walkway—her own.

Alyssa and Brent had been next door neighbors for as long as she could remember. Longer than that actually. Ms. Carter had been her babysitter when Alyssa was still just a baby. That was back when she was Mrs. Carter. After the divorce she had kept the last name but switched to *Ms.* Back then Ms. Carter hadn't worked at the post office. She hadn't worked anywhere. Even after they were old enough for school Alyssa had still gone to the Carter's afterwards. Her entire childhood was a blur of memories that all starred a blond-haired-green-eyed boy.

It was Ms. Carter that taught her how to cook, because Alyssa's own mother was a terrible cook. That didn't matter so much since Mrs. Maddow was a doctor, and when you're a doctor it isn't particularly important if your meals come out of a microwave. Alyssa got tired of frozen dinners by the time she was nine, so she started watching Mrs. Maddow fix dinner. Brent learned too. He said it was stupid girl stuff, but that was better than playing alone.

Brent and Alyssa were the best sort of best friends. They had plenty in common, and even when they didn't they each made the effort to show some interest. So Brent had learned how to cook, and Alyssa had started reading comic books. Her favorite were the X-Men. He teased her mercilessly when she admitted to having a crush on Gambit—the New Orleans bad boy super hero with a Cajun accent. Alyssa might have been more embarrassed, but after all if he told anyone she could always share his dirty little secret—he made the best quiche.

Alyssa let herself into the house, yelled to her dad that she was home, and jogged up the stairs to her room. Alyssa's room had changed a lot over the years. When she was five it was pink and decorated with cute little teddy bears and bunny rabbits. When she was eight her parents took her to a real ballet, and the bunnies and bears were replaced with graceful dancers in pretty tutus. By the time she turned 12 she had convinced her mom to let her repaint the walls a pale shade of green, and the pretty dancers had been replaced by posters of boy bands, and cute TV stars. Now, at 17, those posters were mostly gone too. The walls were still green, but they were decorated instead with photographs. Brent was really getting to be a very good photographer, and she had a lot of his best landscapes framed.

She was pretty sure she'd embarrassed him by insisting he sign and date each print before sealing the frames, but she was serious when she said he would be famous one day. And when he was making millions working for national geographic she could sell her photos, and quit her much less satisfying job in retail. She didn't want to work in retail, but with her skill set (okay her lack of a skill set) it wasn't looking like she'd be finding anything much better than a position at the local sporting goods store anytime soon.

Walking into her room Alyssa toed out of her sneakers, pulled off her cheerleading uniform and pulled on gray sweatpants with her favorite faded Philly Flyers tee-shirt. More comfortable, she crawled onto her bed. What a terrible night. At least it was Friday and there wasn't going to be school in the morning. But there would be school eventually, and when your mom is a doctor you never get to play sick.

Even though it was almost midnight she wasn't tired. Alyssa sat up and looked out her window and into Brent's. Dark. Brent's bedroom window was so close to her own that they had had no trouble hopping back and forth when they were kids. Alyssa's dad put a stop to the window crawling when they started high school. He said it wasn't appropriate anymore given the changes their bodies were going through. Really, he said *changes their bodies were going through*! It was so embarrassing. Also it never really mattered—she still crawled over there occasionally when she was feeling too lazy to walk over the *appropriate* way and use the front door. Alyssa reached for her cell phone and texted her friend.

Alyssa: R U Home

Brent: Nope, why?

Alyssa: just wanted some company, call me later?

Brent: Im on my way see you in 15

She should probably be feeling badly that Brent was cutting his evening short. She knew his curfew wasn't for another hour and a half yet. Brent was eighteen—no driver's license restrictions. Plus his mom was way trusting. Alyssa was pretty sure that even after her birthday in a few months her mom wouldn't raise her midnight-on-weekends-eleven-on-school-nights curfew. Not that her parents were unfair. She could always get curfew extensions for special occasions. And the Carter's house had become sort of exempt from curfew years ago. They knew she was safe there. Anyway Brent was probably on his way home; he wouldn't have left in the middle of anything important.

Suddenly it struck Alyssa as odd that she didn't know where Brent was. Usually, they spent most of their free time together. It was a little strange to think he was off having fun without her. Of course they rarely spent Friday nights together. Not since she'd been old enough to date. And it was dumb for her to think he sat around the house on Friday nights.

Alyssa went to the local public high school and she spent most of her Friday nights out with a boy, or some of her other school friends. Tonight she had been at the football game and then at a party. Brent used to go to school with her, but when they reached high school he was accepted at the Hillfield academy, a pricey private school across town that his dad

3

paid for as part of the divorce agreement. At some point he'd been seeing a girl named Melissa from Hillfield, but he hadn't mentioned her in a couple weeks. She supposed he might have been at a Hillfield football game. Of course the game would have been over a couple hours ago.

"Lyssa?"

Brent's voice sounded muted through the glass. She opened her window and saw his familiar face hanging head and shoulders out of his window.

"Wanna come over?"

"Will it wake your mom up?" Alyssa was already scrambling over her windowsill.

"Nah, she's on a date. Come on." He held out his hand and helped her hop the short distance between the low roofs and climb into his window. "Your parents gonna be worried?"

"Mom's at the hospital and dad never checks on me before bed. Even if he did I'm sure he would call here before panicking."

Brent nodded as he settled himself into his desk chair. Alyssa sat on the floor leaning against his bed and drew her knees to her chest. Brent was fiddling with his lap top, not particularly concerned with playing host to Alyssa. She loved that about their friendship. He never felt the need to force conversation, or change his routine to fit her. She could just sit here enjoying his company while he did whatever he was doing. It looked like he was transferring photos off his camera. Brent's bedroom had changed less over the years. About the same time she painted her walls green, Alyssa convinced him to paint his blue. Originally Brent wanted green because then their rooms would have matched, but in her 12 year old wisdom Alyssa explained that boys liked blue.

So the walls were still blue. And the same cream colored area rug covered most of the hardwood floor in the center of the room. One corner of it was stained purple from a grape Icee they had let melt in its paper cup a few years ago. A bookshelf stood in one corner still crammed full of comics that had gone untouched for years. Any newer books were piled haphazardly on top of the shelf or balanced lengthwise across the rows of comics. Another shelf held a small TV and several video game consoles; the floor directly in front was strewn with game cases. Boys were such slobs. Alyssa crawled over to them and started snapping games back into their cases, and making room for them on a shelf.

"Something wrong Lyssa?"

She turned to find Brent leaned forward in his desk chair, hands propped on his knees, and his eyes trained on her.

Chapter Two

"How can you tell?" Alyssa didn't bother denying her sour mood. There was very little you could hide from someone who had known you all your life.

"You only clean up after me when something's wrong. Things not going too well with Pete?" His tone betrayed an *I told you so* he was clearly fighting to hold back.

Pete was Alyssa's boyfriend. Well her ex-boyfriend. They had been dating since the beginning of the school year. Head cheerleader and captain of the football team—she'd been sure was fate. Brent wasn't so easily convinced. This was probably because Pete had smashed Brent's Batman lunchbox in the fifth grade. At the time Alyssa, of course, had been just as mad as Brent, but that was seven years ago and she figured it was time to let it go.

"We broke up!" Alyssa flounced backwards taking up most of the throw rug with her outstretched limbs.

Brent cocked his head to one side waiting for her to continue. He knew she'd start talking when she was ready to; no point in asking questions until she did.

Alyssa lay where she was for a moment and then rolled onto her side to face him again. "Do you want to make out with me?"

"Sure." Brent looked surprised—and skeptical of her sincerity.

"You don't want to know why?"

"Nope. I'm more of a make out first—ask questions later kinda guy." He winked and wiggled his eyebrows at her.

"It was awful. We went to a party after the game, and I caught him with that slut Lisa Thompson! And I do mean *caught*. He went on and on about why Lisa was so much better for him than I ever was. In front of the whole school!"

"You want I should give him the old one-two?" Brent swung his fists through the air punching imaginary Pete. Alyssa smiled, and almost laughed. Brent always made her feel better.

"No." She sighed and rolled back onto her back. "I'm not all that upset really."

He probably could though, she thought. Brent had always been a little soft and squishy when they were kids, but last year he took a weight lifting class to cover his PE credit for school. And he liked it, so the routine stayed even after the end of term. Actually now that she thought about it Brent was downright attractive. Not that he had been unattractive before, well she hadn't really noticed one way or the other before. He still had the same shaggy blond hair as always and the same green eyes. Only now his arms bulged beneath the fabric of his long sleeved tee shirt, and when he moved the cotton pulled nicely against a flat stomach. He'd traded his glasses for contacts a few weeks ago (a birthday gift from his mom) and now there wasn't anything to draw attention away from his eyes. Which were a very striking shade of green.

"So this is you not upset?" Brent twitched a disbelieving smile at her.

"This is me *humiliated*. First he tried to weasel out of it by accusing me of being hung up on you. He kept saying he wouldn't be surprised if we were sleeping together. When I set him straight about that he started in on how unfeminine I am. Apparently guys don't want to talk sports with their girlfriends. He said no wonder I couldn't even turn you on and that I was probably a lesbian." She paused to take a breath.

"So you think you're a lesbian?" Brent ignored the implied insult to him.

"No, of course not. But if we *were* sleeping together than other people wouldn't think it either!" She was being melodramatic and she knew it. Tomorrow she would think of a realistic solution to her impending social downfall.

T.J. Dell

"So you want to have sex?" Brent took on a bored indulgent tone of voice.

"Be serious for a minute Brent! I am so sure you imagined your first time to be with me, on your floor, and in my old sweats!" He just stared at her. Actually he looked a little surprised "Brent?"

"Okay, so if we aren't going to have sex...wanna play Mario Cart?"

"What was the look for?"

"It's nothing Lyssa." She punched him in the arm. "It just wouldn't be my first time. Not that it was a serious possibility anyway." Brent handed over a controller and settled on the floor against the bed.

"What!"

Brent rolled his eyes. "It isn't a big deal Lyssa"

"No. Of course not. Everyone's having sex, but me! Pete, Lisa, even Brent! Who are you having sex with?"

"At the moment? No one. I am just trying to get a game of Mario Cart going."

Alyssa was undeterred. "Brent! I tell you everything!"

"You're a chick. It's different, chicks talk more."

"Come on—who? Is this a macho thing? Cause you don't have to have to be macho with me."

Brent rolled his eyes again. "I just don't think it would be polite. Anyway we go to different schools Lyssa; I doubt you would know them."

"*Them!* Plural?" Alyssa's eyes went wide. "So you're what? Doing it in the bathroom between classes?"

"Sure, because I go to school in a porno flick. I do date Lyssa. You know...pick the girl up, take her to a movie..." Brent rolled one hand in an et cetera et cetera motion. And then, seeing a genuine measure of anguish on his friend's face, he got serious. "It's cool Alyssa don't let that jackass Pete or anyone else tell you when you're ready."

Alyssa was horrified. "How did I not know this? My best friend is the Hugh Hefner of Pennsylvania." Shaking her head, she picked up her controller. "I am totally gonna own you Carter."

Brent chuckled, acknowledging the end of Alyssa's dramatics.

8

"Is that where you were when I texted you?" Alyssa asked without taking her eyes from the TV.

"Was I having sex? No. I don't think it would have been very good manners to take any calls during sex."

"No, dummy. Were you on a date?"

"Not a good one."

Alyssa nodded, mollified, and concentrated on the screen.

Chapter Three

The next morning Alyssa woke up at 7:00 am despite the fact that she had been with Brent until after 2:00. She was a little sleepy, but staying in bed wouldn't do anything to fix her social problems. Damn Pete. She should have known better—he was basically an ass. But come on! Head cheerleader and the captain of the football team? It should have been perfect. No way was she showing up at school to face that humiliation without some kind of game plan.

Wiping the steam from her bathroom mirror, Alyssa tried to decide if she was prettier than Lisa Thompson. Her brown hair, which her mom called chestnut, hung just past her collar bone. When it dried she knew it would bounce up to graze her shoulders. She liked her hair. She liked her eyes too. Also brown, they were a nice shape—Lisa Thompson had really big eyes. Satisfied with the view Alyssa shimmied into a pair of blue jeans, and a stretchy white turtle neck. She wasn't vain, but she wasn't dumb either and she'd never had any complaints about the way she filled out her cheer uniform. So no way was Lisa Thompson prettier. Showered and changed Alyssa walked back into her room to start strategizing. She screamed.

"Jesus Lyssa!" Brent caught her before she fell backwards.

"Brent. You scared the crap out of me! You can't just crawl through my window—what if my dad caught you."

His face wiggled in an amused way. "I came through the front door; your dad let me in. I just wanted to ask you to go to the corn maze with me today. And I would have called, but you left your cell at my house last night." He held the phone out to her.

"Oh. Well, whatever." Alyssa waved off the moment and took her phone from him. "I can't go today; I have serious angst to suffer through."

"Sounds fun." He commented wryly. "You love the corn maze. We could race."

"You'd lose." Alyssa was starting to waver. "Do you know how popular the corn maze is? It's gonna be crawling with people from school."

"So you are going to hide out here forever? Lame." Brent could tell she was caving. "Come on Chere." He said reaching for his best Cajun accent (and it wasn't very good) "I'll do my Gambit voice all day. One drunken party isn't going to ruin your social standing. C'est la vi."

The Gambit voice did it for her. "All right, but if we see anyone I know…"

"You can hide in the corn." Brent finished for her.

The corn maze was actually one of Alyssa's favorite parts of the fall. The town really went all out with a huge corn maze, lots of food vendors, hay rides, games, and all sorts of other fun stuff. The maze itself was always really impressive. They advertized an average of 90 minutes to find your way out. Alyssa usually made it in 45. Most years she went so many times that by the end of the season she could walk through it blind folded. One year Brent had bet against her doing just that and at the end of that day Alyssa was the owed one homemade quiche. She hadn't gotten around to it this year yet though. And the season was half way over. Being seniors was extremely time-absorbing. Plus Pete hadn't been interested. Really Pete had only been interested in one thing—something Lisa Thompson was a little freer with than Alyssa.

"So did you really want to race?" Brent slung his camera over one shoulder as he climbed out of the car.

"Nah, but let's get some hot chocolate before we go in. It's freezing out here." She wasn't wrong. Halloween was still a two and a half weeks away but the temperature was dipping dangerously closer to icy every morning.

"Ooh yeah, and some of those cinnamon roasted cashews too." Draping his free arm around her neck they headed off for their snacks.

The line for hot chocolate was pretty long, so they agreed Brent would go get the roasted cashews and come back. "Au revoir Chere" Brent winked at her and walked off towards another line.

"Alyssa! Who's the French guy?"

Alyssa turned around to find Jennifer Pastings and another girl from school waiting in line behind her. Jennifer was the biggest gossip—and she had had a front row seat to the previous night's events.

"Hey Jenn, what French guy?"

"Don't play coy with me Alyssa Maddow! You've been holding out—he's a hottie."

Alyssa smiled. Brent was pretty hot these days, and she was happy for him. "Yeah he is. You remember Brent. He went to middle school with us."

"That's Brent Carter? No way! He's sure been eating his Wheaties." Both girls turned their heads straining to find him in the crowd.

"That is super sexy. Chere is 'sweet' right? I didn't even know he was French." The other girl, who Alyssa couldn't have named if her English grade depended on it, spoke up.

"Not French, ladies,—Cajun." Brent reappeared holding a large paper cone filled to the brim with sweet smelling roasted cashews. "And I'm not—it's just my little pet name for Lyssa. Sort of an old joke we have." Brent gave them an amiable look while he offered around the snack. "How are you Jenny? Sue?"

Sue! Of course that was her name.

"Bre-ent" Jennifer was purring. "What have you been up to?"

"Same as you I imagine. Just in a jacket and tie. I'm at Hillfield." Jennifer was flirting—and Brent was flirting back! Alyssa very much wished the corn maze was closer so she could hide. As it was, sprinting 50 yards before darting into the stalks would probably make a spectacle.

When they'd paid for their hot chocolates Alyssa and Brent headed for the corn maze. It was fairly obvious that Jennifer wanted to tag along, but Alyssa didn't invite her. Inside, the corn stalks were tall enough to throw them into shadows. Wind was kept at bay by the thick growth making the pathways warmer. Not *take off your hats and gloves* warm, but more comfortable than the open fields. Alyssa took the lead and they walked in silence awhile with her making sure turns and Brent snapping occasional photos. Alyssa considered asking him what the visual appeal of a bunch of dried up old corn could be, but she knew better than to question his muse.

"You were flirting with Jenn." Alyssa said after several minutes.

"Was I?"

"You know you were. I just want to know why. She's not a very nice person—actually she's kind of a bitch."

"I remember." Brent sighed. "I wasn't flirting Lyssa. I was just saying hello. Why are you being so weird? You're not jealous are you?"

Alyssa stopped short and reversed directions past the last fork they had taken. Wisely, Brent followed. "No." She answered honestly. "I'm not being weird. I'm just trying to think. I have to go to school with those girls on Monday, they were both at the party last night, and they are pretty major tongue waggers."

"I think you are worrying too much Lyssa. Maybe you should try and care a little less about what other people are thinking or saying."

Alyssa snorted. "Boys." She shook her head. "Don't people talk at that school of yours?"

"Of course, but I don't have to listen. You know I hate gossip; aren't we getting too old for that crap?"

Typical Brent, Alyssa thought. And she decided to give up. He either couldn't or wouldn't understand the all consuming awfulness of an entire school knowing the intimate details of your rejection. To punish him for not understanding, Alyssa took three extra wrong turns.

By the time they reached the exit gates she had forgiven him—mostly because he let her finish the last of the cashews. "Hay ride? Or there's pumpkin bowling this year." Brent crumpled their garbage and tossed it into a nearby trash barrel.

"Pumpkin bowling?" Alyssa inquired doubtfully.

"Come on Chere, where's your sense of adventure?" Brent grabbed her wrist and towed her off in the direction of the makeshift bowling lanes.

"Alyssa?"

Brent and Alyssa both turned around to find Pete trotting over to them. Behind him stood a group of guys from the football team, all laughing and shouting after him.

"Alyssa! Let's talk." Pete was slightly out of breath when he reached them. "I was a little drunk last night. I think I could have been nicer."

Alyssa fixed him with a disbelieving look.

"Okay. I was a lot drunk. But I didn't mean for you to find out about Lisa that way. I just thought...you know homecoming is in a few weeks."

"You were waiting to tell me after homecoming!" Shock spurred her into speaking.

"It's not like you left me much choice, babe. Two months is a long time to *wait for you to get comfortable*. Or maybe you really have been more comfortable than I thought." His eyes settled on Brent's hand still wrapped around her wrist.

"Pete—I didn't..." Alyssa trailed off too angry and hurt to keep talking.

"Oh! Pete!" Brent made an exaggerated gesture as if just realizing who this guy was. Dropping Alyssa's wrist Brent held out his hand. "Brent Carter. Nice to meet you."

Pete shook hands with a shocked expression that only got more shocked when Brent withdrew his arm and wrapped it across Alyssa's shoulders. "Yeah—I know we went to middle school together." Pete found his voice.

"Did we?" Brent responded as he began twisting a section of Alyssa's hair. "Sorry. I don't remember."

"Sure you do. Pete Edser? I play football?" Pete puffed himself up a bit as he recovered. "Or maybe you don't, you always seemed to be buried in a comic book."

"Hmm?" Brent was nuzzling Alyssa's ear. "Oh yeah, I did have quite the comic book collection." He didn't even turn his head when he answered. "How bout that pumpkin bowling? I'll win you a prize." He whispered to Alyssa—loud enough for Pete to know the conversation had come to an end.

Brent steered a still stunned Alyssa back around walking her toward the pumpkin bowling. Pete stared after them.

"I have always hated that guy." Brent bit off when they were out of ear shot.

"And I thought you didn't recognize him." Alyssa elbowed him teasingly. "You were perfect! What happened to being too old for gossip and not caring what others think?"

"I don't Lyssa. But that doesn't mean I want you to sign up for doormat classes either. What were you doing with that guy?"

"Not much—that was the problem, remember?"

Brent didn't respond. Suddenly he needed all his attention to be focused on the small pumpkin barreling down the lane towards pins painted to look like corn cobs. It must have worked because when they left that afternoon Alyssa had two big stuffed bears.

Chapter Four

Monday morning Alyssa dragged her feet. It took her twice as long as usual to shower and dry her hair, and then she needed to find the perfect how-could-anyone-want-Lisa-more-than-me outfit. The result was worth the extra effort though. Her clingy knee length chocolate colored skirt made the most of her legs—not that anyone would be looking at her legs while she was wearing her burnt gold sweater with the extra scoopy scoop neck. She was totally an autumn.

It wasn't really her style to be so dressy for a Monday and she would surely be regretting her skinny heel ankle boots by fourth period, but if people were going to be staring she was going to give them something worth staring at. Feeling pretty good about herself, she didn't even let the rain bother her as she dashed to her car. Her mood however took a quick plunge when she couldn't start her car. It was the third time this month. Maybe she should buy a new battery? Hers was the only car in the drive—her dad must have left for work already. Frustrated, Alyssa screamed and banged her fists against the steering wheel.

"Okay in there?" There was a knock on the driver's window. Brent was bent over witnessing her melt down. Even though he was holding an umbrella she could tell he was getting wet. The maroon of his Hillfield blazer was spotted along his back with rain drops.

She opened the door two inches. "I think the battery died…what do you know about cars?"

"Not a lot. Come on I'll give you a lift." Alyssa climbed out of her car and huddled under his umbrella as they walked to his.

"Won't you be late?" She asked when she'd climbed into the passenger seat.

Brent checked the clock as he pulled onto the road. "It'll be close, but we start later than you and my homeroom teacher likes me, so it's cool." He glanced over and gave her kind of an up-down with his eyes. "What's up? Is it dress up day at school or something?"

"No. Do I look good?"

He ignored her question. "Is this about Pete? You think a fancy dress is gonna have him crawling back?"

"It's a skirt, not a dress. And no—I don't want Pete to come crawling back. Well the crawling bit would be fun to watch, but I'm no one's doormat."

Brent smiled. "Good. But why so dressed up?"

"This is just how I'm dressed. You are used to a school with uniforms."

"Ok—ay." He was smirking at her.

"It's true!"

"Lyssa, you ate breakfast at my house last Monday."

"So?"

"So. You were wearing a busted old pair of blue jeans, and your Flyers tee shirt."

"Shut up."

Brent did. And he stayed that way until he pulled in front of her school.

"Where are you going?" Alyssa asked when she saw him reach for his door handle.

"You don't have an umbrella." He said simply as he opened his and walked to the around the passenger side. "Shake a leg Maddow—I'm gonna be late."

Alyssa would have said something smart back, but she could tell he was joking. And she really didn't want to get any wetter than necessary. Safely underneath the overhang of the school's entrance, Alyssa turned to face him. "Thanks. I'll get a ride home with Beth." She was on the squad with Alyssa, and they had practice together after school anyway.

Brent nodded. "Rent a movie later? I'll cook."

"Hockey game's on at seven. But if you're still willing to cook you can come watch it on our big screen. Dad's been ordering a lot of pizza. I am in serious danger of turning into a pepperoni."

"Pittsburgh's playing—you hate Pittsburgh."

"I know, I wanna watch 'em lose." Alyssa flashed her brightest smile.

Brent chuckled. "kay. See ya around 6:15." He tweaked a strand of her hair and hurried back to his car.

Alyssa turned around to see half a dozen kids from her class trying to look as though they weren't staring. Not bothering to pretend about staring was Jenn, and she was headed straight for her.

"Alyssa! Wow. He's even hotter in that uniform. I might have to get me a Hillfield man. I never would have thought you could trade up from Pete Edser, but I think I've been fishing in the wrong pond."

"Jenn, you know Brent and I have been friends forever." Alyssa tried to move past her.

"Oh no, you don't. I could tell something was going on when I saw you two together Saturday, and now he's driving you to school? Well I'm glad you didn't waste any time. It could have made things awkward you know—with Pete and Lisa together and you all alone." Jennifer's sugar sweet voice was probably supposed to sound sympathetic, but piranhas tend to have a hard time pulling off sympathetic. "And don't you look nice. Dressed up for you new man? I'm glad. All those *sportsy* clothes? Not really a good look for you."

"I think it's romantic." Alyssa hadn't even noticed Sue until she spoke up. She practically melted into Jenn's shadow. No wonder Alyssa'd had trouble remembering the girl's name. "Him pining away for you all these years, and now you're available, and he got all sexy and stuff."

"Is that how it was?" Jenn was talking again. "I bet he looks yummy in a suit. It will be a tight fit in the limo, but I'm glad things worked out for you."

"What?" Alyssa was getting a head ache.

"The homecoming dance silly. Or don't you think you'll be able to keep him that long?" There were the teeth Alyssa had come to expect from Jenn.

"Of course we'll be at the dance. I just hadn't decided if we wanted to share a limo. I suppose we will though. If there is a problem with space I can just sit in Brent's lap." Alyssa walked away. Not as fast as too be running away. But fast enough to keep from hyperventilating in front of her friends. Brent was really not gonna like this.

At 6:15 on the dot Brent showed up at Alyssa's back door carrying a grocery bag. He wasn't in a good mood though. Alyssa needed to ask him to ask her to the homecoming dance, but this was clearly not the time. He was all but silent as he made the pasta and chopped veggies for the salad. When Alyssa asked him what he'd like to drink, he pretty much growled his answer. Definitely not the time to ask for a favor.

"Food's good. Thanks." Alyssa broke the silence after they'd been sitting at her kitchen table for several uncomfortable moments.

He grunted.

"Something wrong grouchy pants?" She decided to tease him out of his bad mood.

"How was school today Lyssa?"

"Erm...not as bad as I expected?" Was she busted?

"I got an interesting phone call a little while ago. Betsy Mink doesn't think it's a good idea for her and I to go to a movie this weekend after all— but she is happy for us. Anything you want to tell me?" Yup. She was busted.

"Mink? As in Theresa Mink?" Theresa was in Alyssa's chemistry class.

"I think that's her cousin. What's going on Lyssa?"

"Sorry!" Alyssa moaned and dropped her head into her hands. "Jennifer kind of had the idea that we were a couple. And she just kept going on and on about how great it was that I wasn't going to make things awkward for Pete and Lisa. And she thinks you're hot!"

Brent shot her a look that clearly said he could care less about the last part. So Alyssa hurried on.

"It's your fault anyway! All that touchy-feely stuff at the corn maze, and then holding the umbrella this morning…"

"Okay, I may have given Pete the wrong impression to take him down a peg or two, and yeah I held your umbrella—which I would have done for anybody dumb enough to go out in the rain without their own umbrella—but you could have set her straight."

"Did you really like Betsy?"

"What? No. That's fine, but I don't like her thinking I asked her out and then hooked up with you a couple days later."

"Please do this for me Brent. Going to homecoming alone would be worse than not going at all. And not going is not an option!"

"I would have taken you to the damn dance Lyssa! I just don't see why we have to pretend it's something it isn't."

"I don't want people thinking I'm alone that's all."

"Yeah, I can see where that would be a real tragedy." Brent fixed her with a condescending look. "Look, I could care less about the game. I've got homework to do." He got up to leave.

"Brent!"

"Its fine Lyssa, I'll take you to the dance. I will even play prince charming if you think that will make you happy."

"Thanks. But actually I was going to ask you for a ride to school in the morning. Dad took my car to the mechanic."

"Yeah, okay. I don't want to be late though so we'll have to leave early. 'Night." Brent left, and Alyssa tried to watch the game alone. The Penguins got crushed, but she couldn't really enjoy it.

Chapter Five

Brent ended up dropping Alyssa off at school the rest of the week. He was polite and sometimes even funny, but for the first time in 17 years things were awkward between them. She hadn't spent so many evenings alone since the tenth grade when she was banned from the Carter household until Brent recovered from mono. Even then he had called her every day. Suddenly Brent had too much homework to do any hanging out with her.

"There's a football game tonight, right?" Brent was pulling into a spot at her school on Friday morning. "I thought I would come and watch you cheer."

"Oh. Okay, thanks. The game's at 5:00, but…you don't have too."

"Well I don't have a date anymore—remember?" Brent tossed her a smile, but it didn't make her laugh. It wasn't his real smile.

"Umm…there's a party too."

"I figured as much. Lyssa, are you sure this is what you want? Wouldn't it be easier to stop all this pretending?"

"Not really." Alyssa muttered and got out of the car. She didn't want to give him a chance to change his mind.

Alyssa plastered on her brightest smile during the game. She cheered and jumped for all she was worth—even when Pete made two touch downs, and she would rather have booed. Brent spent most of the game propped against a railing, cheering when they scored, chatting occasionally with other kids, and generally playing the good boyfriend. For some reason it made Alyssa feel even worse when he smiled and waved at her after their halftime routine.

The party was a little better. Alyssa and Brent had been to tons of parties together. And even though he hadn't seen a lot of these people in several years Brent had no problem fitting in and making conversation. Alyssa really envied that about him. He was comfortable in just about any situation. Everywhere they went he seemed to make friends. It was no different in a house full of teenagers that, Alyssa knew, would turn on him in a second if it benefitted them socially.

"Bre-ent" Jennifer sidled up to where they were standing. "Twice in one week, are you following me?" She put one slinky manicured hand on his forearm. Alyssa wasn't jealous, but she did have an urge to break each of those fingers.

Brent took a discreet half-step backwards slipping one arm around Alyssa until his hand settled possessively low on her hip. "Jenny. Good game wasn't it?"

"It was a good game. Pete really pulled us out of the fire with that last play." Jenn paused clearly expecting some kind of reaction—anything to feed her rumor habit. She didn't get one. Brent stared at her for a few long moments and then smiled slightly when she walked away.

"How do you do that?" Alyssa twisted around to look at him.

"What did I do?"

"You always know exactly what to say or I guess what not to say. I would have been furious with her. I would have mentioned Pete's fumble at the very least."

Brent sighed. He seemed to be sighing at her a lot lately. "It isn't what I'm doing Lyssa. It is something I'm not doing. I'm not that guy. I don't need to take someone else down to feel better about myself. And it matters exactly zero to me what that sad pathetic girl thinks."

Alyssa's jaw dropped open. She was very sure that she'd been insulted, and there was nothing she could do about it.

"Oh that's sweet, they are gonna kiss!" A girl's voice sounded out from the sea of teenagers and half the heads in the room focused on where Alyssa looked to be twisted in Brent's embrace.

She gave him a pleading look, and he rolled his eyes at her. The eye rolling thing was getting pretty popular too. "Show's over guys—get your own girl." He called out with a good natured smile and led Alyssa out a door into the back yard.

Someone Alyssa thought might be in her English class was standing by a cooler and he handed her a beer. Brent waved his off.

"Since when do you drink beer?" Brent muttered as they walked on.

"I drink." She was beginning to wish they'd gone straight home after the game.

"Sure wine at thanksgiving, champagne at new years. But you hate beer."

"I only have one when I come to these things. It is easier that way." They had come to a stop at the fence. Even in the dark she could see disappointment in his eyes. He sighed deeply and then swept her in front of him so her back was pressed to the fence post. His face lowered to an inch from hers and one hand slipped down her arm until he wrapped it around her hand still holding the beer can. Anyone in the yard would be able to see a couple making out in the shadows. He tipped their hands and the beer can sideways spilling its contents into the grass.

"There." He whispered as he straightened up.

"Head's up!" A football came spiraling towards them; Brent turned just in time to make the catch. Some of the guys from the team were playing a game of drunken catch. Brent joined them while Alyssa curled up in the grass, holding her empty can, with the other girlfriends.

Beth sat down with her. "So, Brent Carter huh? What's up with that?"

"Oh you know—it umm just happened." Alyssa hedged.

"Okay." Beth nodded her head. "I gotta say—I never really got you and Pete. Brent's cool though. I used to have kind of a crush on him you know…in the eighth grade. But hey, no worries. Tommy asked me to the homecoming dance."

Alyssa wasn't super surprised. Tommy and Beth were kind of a no brainer. At parties he was always bringing her drinks, and during the games she cheered the loudest when he had the ball. "That's great Beth. You guys will have a lot of fun." Beth chattered on about Tommy for a few minutes, but Alyssa was having trouble focusing on the conversation. Eventually Beth wandered off to find someone else to talk to.

At the end of the night Brent walked her to her door. "Thanks I appreciated this." She said.

Brent's forehead wrinkled up, and he shook his head. "This is usually when the girl tells me *thanks I had fun.*"

"Fine. I had fun." Alyssa flashed her date-smile at him.

"No you didn't Lyssa. Is there a cheer competition tomorrow?"

"Yes."

"Should I be there?"

"You never come to my cheer meets."

Brent rolled his eyes. "Would Pete have been there?"

"Nope. You are off the hook."

"Kay. Let's do something after then. Just the two of us?"

Alyssa nodded and walked through the door. That would be good, she thought. Mixing Brent in with her school life was throwing off her balance. How could she have known it would be this way? People liked her! Half the girls at the party tonight wanted to be her! So why when she let Brent see that girl did she feel as though she'd been found lacking? Where everyone else saw a happy popular pretty cheerleader he seemed to see nothing. She went to bed thinking that maybe she should have had that beer.

Chapter Six

Saturday afternoon Alyssa was in a bit of a rush to get home. All the other girls were going out for pizza to celebrate their win. Alyssa usually would have been happy to join them. Beth wanted to go shopping—she still needed a dress for the dance, and maybe they could hang out at her house after. None of that held any interest for her.

As quickly as she could, Alyssa shed her cheer uniform, scrubbed the glitter from her face, and pulled on more comfortable clothes. Just as she was tugging a green sweater over her head, her phone buzzed. It was Brent.

"Hey, you wanna take a walk with me? It's warmer today than it has been, could be the last good day."

"Okay, sure. Meet you out front in ten?"

"Kay."

"I thought you wanted to take a walk?" Alyssa was surprised to see Brent's car pulled up to the curb in front of her house.

"I wanted to go down to the pond. Those trees still have their leaves." Brent held up his camera bag as part of his explanation. The pond was almost big enough to qualify as a lake. It was a very popular gathering place in warm weather, but they would most likely have the area to themselves in October.

And they did. Brent's car was alone in the parking lot when they started trekking around the edge of the pond to the strip of trees growing at the far end. They walked quietly, and it seemed that the week's stress hadn't affected their relationship too badly. Alyssa still felt more comfortable with Brent than anywhere else in the world. He began snapping photos the closer they got to the trees.

They were pretty enough. Still half full of colorful leaves and the pond was icy smooth providing a mirror effect. Alyssa lagged back watching her friend work. She never would have thought twice about the beauty in front of her if not for Brent. She knew without a doubt there would be another photo on her wall soon. When they crossed into the tree line Brent began aiming his camera up into the trees. Above them the afternoon sun was winking in and out from behind branches. It was truly beautiful. Alyssa stood for awhile admiring a view she never would have noticed alone.

"I can't wait to see them. You are a total artist about this stuff."

"Thanks." Brent barely nodded slightly in her direction as he continued on.

Alyssa wasn't insulted though. He was just like this when he got behind a camera. Completely absorbed. No, she wasn't insulted—maybe a little jealous though. It must be nice to have something that makes you happy that way. Something that consumes all your concentration—an escape from the every day. Maybe she should get a hobby. Not that she had time for one.

As warm as it was, October hadn't completely surrendered and the air bit at Alyssa's skin. Looking around for something to distract her from the weather, her eyes rested on something dirty but glossy at the edge of the path. Someone had abandoned a couple of water bottles on the trail, and further down Alyssa picked up an empty trail mix bag. Alyssa followed along behind Brent picking up the stray bit of litter for another 45 or so minutes. By the time he was ready to head back Alyssa was holding the hem of her sweater out creating a net to carry her findings.

Back in the parking lot Alyssa emptied her arms into a trash can. Behind her she heard she shutter of Brent's camera clicking. "Thinking of branching off into garbage?" She asked him when she turned to find the camera trained on her.

"No. Just practicing."

Alyssa tilted her head, puzzled.

"I have a *living art* project coming up in my photography class and I'm not too good at *people pictures*. I was thinking of cheating and using a series exploring the changing of the seasons." He waved towards the trees. "But that's a cop out. I know Mr. Arnold will call me out on it."

"So it has to be a picture of a person?"

"Or an animal and it has to be a series of photos." Brent packed his camera away and switched it for a football in the trunk of his car. Tossing the ball back and forth between them, they headed back to the open field while the talked. Brent wasn't the athlete Alyssa was, but he didn't mind throwing the ball around. "Actually I was hoping you might do me a favor—would you be my subject?"

"Like pose for the camera?" Alyssa stuck her best cheerleader pose, and sparkled her cheeriest smile at him.

"Nah, that doesn't seem very organic." He quirked a smile at her. "Just let me tote my camera around with us for a couple of weeks. "Should be pretty easy. You always photograph really well.

"Because I'm so pretty?"

Brent shook his head; laughing, he reached back and threw the ball deep.

Alyssa got too close the edge of the water, and her feet flew out from under her, kicking up a shower of mud. She was scrambling out of the icy brown water when Brent reached her.

"I'm so sorry Lyssa—are you okay?" There was real concern on his face, but he couldn't help snickering a little when he saw her mud splattered face.

"Just peachy! This water is freezing!" She wasn't really as mad as she sounded. "But I got the ball." She held out the football (also sloppy with mud) as she crawled back to the solid ground.

"Congratulations, you just won the Carter/Maddow sports challenge." Brent quipped, helping her to her feet.

"You must mean Maddow/Carter." Her words shook because her teeth were beginning to chatter.

"Come on champ. Let's get you dried off." They both headed back to the car laughing.

Brent pulled clean sweatpants and a tee shirt from the gym bag in his trunk. And, like the gentleman he was, he turned his back while Alyssa changed behind the car. There wasn't much they could do about her wet hair, but Brent turned the heat on full blast the whole drive home.

"I really am sorry Lyssa. I hope you don't get sick." Brent was shouting so Alyssa would hear him through the closed bathroom door and over the sound of water spraying. Alyssa was taking a hot shower and Brent had just finished putting her muddy clothes in the washer.

"Don't worry about it. That 'getting sick from cold weather' bit is an old wives tale—mom's a doctor remember?" Alyssa yelled back to him.

"Kay. I'm gonna run home and grab my laptop. I'll come back and we can watch the hockey game together."

Chapter Seven

"Pop?" Alyssa shouted as she walked through her grandfather's door with Brent right behind her.

Most Sundays Alyssa drove over to the retirement home to visit with her grandfather. Pop complained a lot about having to live with 'all those old geezers', but she suspected he was happier now than when he'd been in his house all alone. When she was younger her dad brought her to visit on weekends. Sometimes he still joined her, but more often than not he stayed home. Alyssa's Dad and Pop didn't always get along super well. When her dad made his excuses Alyssa would often call Brent.

Pop loved Brent. Because Brent could, sometimes, beat him at chess. That was a good enough reason all by itself to bring Brent. Alyssa loved her Pop, but she was terrible at chess. Pop used to go easy on her, but now that she was older she had to take her lumps like a grown up. Chess is super hard. This day was one of those days when her dad wasn't interested in visiting and Brent cheerfully agreed to join her.

Stoneybrook retirement community was very pretty. All the buildings were surrounded by well manicured lawns and gardens—and all those lawns and gardens were filled with pretty ornamental benches. Alyssa often wondered if this was because old people liked walks, even though they needed to rest every ten feet. Over the years Pop had been in several rooms. It seemed that every year or two he would have heart troubles and be moved to a different room on a different floor with more nurses. All the rooms were really nice though. And there were pretty common rooms on every floor. On Wednesdays Pop was in a Wii bowling league that met in his common room. His team was in second place.

Alyssa and Brent took awhile to reach Pop's room. Every corner or alcove they passed on their way to Pop's room was crammed with fancy old fashioned chairs and sofas. Sometimes those sofas would be filled with familiar faces. Weekly visits made Alyssa a very popular person at Stoneybrook. Charles at the nurse's station wanted to know if she thought the Flyers had a chance this season. Of course they did! Mrs. Sloan stopped her to show off pictures from her grandson's wedding, and Mr. Petry needed help with his neck tie.

"Thanks Miss Alyssa, I gotta look my best tonight. Gotta date with Sofia you know!"

Mr. Petry ate dinner with Sofia Bunch every Sunday night, and every Sunday night he was brimming with excitement. Alyssa thought this was the sweetest thing she'd ever seen, and anyway she could tie a tie pretty well. Brent hung back a little today. His camera clicked away making Alyssa a little nervous.

Eventually they reached Pop's room. The brass plaque beside the number 718 read: Alistair Maddow. Like always the door itself was open and the sounds of a baseball game could be heard in the hallway. Pop liked ESPN Classic and he didn't like his hearing aid.

"Pop?"

"I hear you!" The TV in the sitting area clicked off, and Pop appeared from around a corner. "You're late today."

"Sorry." Alyssa mostly disregarded his animosity—Pop was only cranky on the outside. Walking over to him, she hugged him lightly and kissed his wrinkled cheek.

"Good to see you Lyssa. Steven." Pop's eyes clouded over when he reached out to shake hands with Brent. Steven was Alyssa's father's name.

"Pop, this is Brent." Alyssa corrected him gently. "You remember Brent." It was only lately that he'd been getting confused, and most days he was as sharp as ever. It made her heartsick to see him this way. When she was younger Pop had taken her fishing, taught her to play ball, and how to throw a punch better than any boy she'd ever met. Now, sometimes, he seemed so old.

"Of course I remember." His voice was sharp. "You look different boy."

"I'm sure I do, sir. I'm not wearing my glasses." Brent agreed easily. As if he hadn't been to visit several times since getting contacts. And as if the absence of those glasses could suddenly make him lose three inches of height, and gain twenty pounds—not to mention age him thirty years. "How's your bowling game?"

"You should see these old geezers trying to bowl on that TV. Terrible." Pop's face lit up proudly. "Bowled a 274 last week. Never did so well at the real thing."

"Congratulations." Brent lowered himself into a chair and gestured to the chess board that always sat at the ready on a small table. "Would you care for a game?"

Brent and Pop played chess for a little over an hour. Alyssa curled up in an easy chair to watch. All the while the three of them chatted. Pop asked Alyssa about school, and cheerleading. They spent a good bit of time dissecting the Flyers game from the day before. Pop thought they'd played sloppy and were lucky that St. Louis played sloppier. Alyssa was inclined to agree. Brent figured a win was a win, but he was concentrating too hard on the board in front of him to mention it.

When the game was over—Pop crushed Brent—it was just about time for Pop to go down to dinner.

"Well played Mr. Maddow. I will have to practice before I visit again." Brent picked his camera bag up.

Pop snorted. "How old are you now, boy?"

"I was eighteen last month sir."

"Well then you're a man now, bout time you started calling me Al. You take care of my girl here now—promise?"

"Yes sir." Brent shook his hand.

"I don't need taking care of Pop." Embarrassed, Alyssa chided him. "See you next week, okay?" With a hug and a kiss the two friends left him to get ready for his dinner.

"Sorry about that." Alyssa said when they'd reached the hall.

"About what?" Brent wrinkled his face, confused. "I like your grandfather, Lyssa. But I am starting to think he must have been letting me win sometimes. I really got my butt handed to me today."

Alyssa snorted—a lot like her Pop had. "No, way. Pop doesn't believe in *letting* people win. If he did I wouldn't mind playing so much."

Going to school was easier the following week. Alyssa had her car back, so there wasn't any reason for Brent to be mixing with her school life; the weekend had really helped her restore that much needed balance to her life. At lunch on Monday Beth was full of news about the dress she'd bought on Saturday, and about how she was glad it was blue because blue was Tommy's favorite color. The table of cheerleaders erupted into discussion of dress colors, styles, and prices.

"What is Brent's favorite color?" Jennifer asked sweetly the seat next to Alyssa.

"Brent likes green." Alyssa was getting very tired of Jennifer.

"Oh, my dress is green you know." Jennifer mentioned casually—although her casualness was betrayed by the catty look in her eyes. Jennifer was going to the dance with John, or Jake, or James—Alyssa was pretty sure it was some J name.

And not that she was jealous, but Alyssa didn't like the idea of Brent admiring Jennifer's dress. Maybe she should rethink her own coffee colored gown. Except she really liked its beaded neck line. No, she loved her dress and she wasn't going to let Jenn get to her. This decision made Alyssa feel quite Brent-like and proud of herself. Until Jenn started asking about how they'd spent the weekend; and commenting on how convenient it must be to have him right next door. Alyssa accidentally knocked her juice into Jenn's lap.

"She's so jealous." Beth offered later. "I bet Jeff will hate her dress."

Jeff! Why was it so hard for her to remember the names of Jenn's minions? "I don't care if she is jealous. I just wish she'd keep it to herself."

"You're right. Brent wouldn't do that to you. He's not Pete."

Alyssa decided not to mention that, while Brent was extremely trustworthy, that wasn't why she wasn't jealous. All this pretending was starting to get annoying.

"Are you going to be at the hospital on Thursday?" Beth asked after Alyssa had been quiet for awhile.

The varsity club was sponsoring a fall carnival for the children's wing of the local hospital. They had done one the year before and it had gone so well they'd decided to make it an annual event. "Yeah. I think I am in charge of bobbing for apples."

"That sounds fun. I'm at the Jack-o-lantern table. We should have signed up together. We could have been at the same booth."

"That would have been good." Beth's relaxed comment startled her a little. She really enjoyed Beth's company, but they didn't usually go out of their way to spend time together. Probably because I am always so busy with Brent, Alyssa thought. Also she thought it was kind of a shame. Having a close girlfriend would be nice; next time Beth wanted to go shopping Alyssa resolved to make the time. "What about Tommy—I think he did the jack-o-lanterns last year."

"Well the sign ups were before we were together, so he's in charge of one of the games. We are riding over together though. Is Brent coming?"

"Oh, I hadn't really thought to ask him." Alyssa stammered. Her last attempt at mixing her two worlds had hardly been a stellar success.

"I know he doesn't go here—but I am sure the hospital won't turn away his help."

"You're probably right. I'll mention it to him. But he's been really busy lately with some class work so…" Alyssa let the sentence drop. It was a pretty lame excuse anyway. She would have to ask him now. Maybe she could try buttering him up first—let him beat her at Mario Cart? And it might be helpful if she showed up with some sort of bribe. Where could she get cinnamon roasted cashews on a Monday afternoon?

Chapter Eight

"Am I going to regret accepting these?" Brent joked when he opened the door. Alyssa was smiling and holding out a paper cone brimming with, now slightly cold, cinnamon roasted cashews. It was Wednesday. Alyssa talked herself into putting off seeing him until the last minute, but she was going to suck it up and ask him today—since the carnival was in less than 24 hours.

"What? A girl can't just stop at the corn maze and buy her best friend overpriced seasonal snack foods?" Alyssa walked past him and into his family room when he took the cashews from her.

"Well gee, when you put it that way..." The rest of his sarcasm was lost when he downed a handful of the cashews before emptying the rest into a bowl.

Alyssa was ignoring him anyway. Sitting on the floor she began unpacking her back pack onto his coffee table and pulling out her calculus homework. "I need you to help me with my homework."

"You're an ace at math, Lyssa. What do you really need?"

"Well well, Mister Smarty-pants, it just so happens that I don't need help with calculus. I just thought I would start on my math homework while you proof read my Shakespeare paper." Alyssa was pulling a second folder from her back pack and held this one out to her friend.

Brent nodded. He didn't apologize, but he did take the paper. English was Brent's best subject, but he knew Alyssa struggled just to maintain the C she needed to qualify for cheerleading. Sitting on the couch Brent put their snack on the coffee table and began to read. They worked separately for the better part of an hour. Occasionally Brent would comment aloud on her paper, but he mostly made notes in the margin for her to use later. When he finished that he moved on to his own homework. And they kept working quietly until Ms. Carter served dinner.

"Alyssa! We haven't seen you for dinner lately. Where have you been hiding?" Ms. Carter commented as she spooned homemade beef stew into three bowls.

"Oh I guess I've just been busy. Senior year you know."

"I do know. Brent's been busy too. It seems like just yesterday I was taking you two to story time at the library and watching you play tag in the back yard. Now you're seniors and soon you'll be graduating…"

"Mom…" Brent groaned. Alyssa giggled. Ms. Carter could sometimes be very sentimental. It embarrassed Brent, but Alyssa's parents weren't sentimental at all and she thought it was nice.

"Okay! Okay!" Ms. Carter held up her hands in defeat. "Any who, Alyssa, tell me about the carnival at the hospital. I hear it is going to be even bigger this year. What a wonderful thing you are doing for those kids."

"What carnival?" Brent's eyes were wide as he listened to his mother ramble. "I didn't know you were doing something at the hospital." He turned to Alyssa.

"Oh. Well we did it last year too—the Varsity club at school that is. But you were already at your dad's for the holidays so…Anyway we are doing it earlier this year, tomorrow actually. Umm. I thought you might want to come with me?"

"Shakespeare paper my ass." Brent mumbled as he went back to his dinner.

"That's a great idea!" Ms. Carter took no notice of the tension at the dinner table as she continued on about what a great contribution they were making to society and what socially responsible adults they were growing into. Alyssa hardly tasted her stew.

"Really, Lyssa?" Brent finally spoke again after they'd finished the dishes and he was walking her to her front door. "This is getting outrageous. You never needed bribes or excuses to talk to me before. I would love to help at the hospital. I would have done it anyway you know. Even without the boyfriend pretense."

"It wasn't an excuse. You know how bad I am doing in that class! If I don't keep my grade up I won't be able to cheer in the spring." Alyssa shuffled her feet and refused to look him in the eyes. She shouldn't have asked him. She could have thought of something to tell Beth.

"Don't split hairs Lyssa. It was an excuse. Not in all of our lives have you ever needed an excuse to come over before. Is this really how you want to spend our senior year? Everything is going to change soon, and you are missing what's left of high school. And now you are making me miss it too."

"What are you talking about!?" Alyssa was pretty sure she would be embarrassed later for shouting in the middle of the street.

"You. Us. This whole juvenile I-have-a-boyfriend nonsense. You are so important to me Lyssa, but this fake boyfriend bit is getting old. And it is making things weird with us." Brent started pacing a small circle in front of her walk. "Maybe, it wouldn't be so bad you know if you didn't cheer in the spring."

"What! What is it you have against cheerleading? You weren't happy when I got chosen for head cheerleader, and you've never bothered to come to my meets."

"I would come to the meets if it mattered to you, but it doesn't. You don't even like cheering! Why aren't you playing softball, or soccer? I would be at every game."

"You don't know what you're talking about."

"I know enough. I know this isn't really you." Brent held up a hand ticking off his points on his fingers. "You hate cheerleading. You had a boyfriend you never liked, you have a crowd of friends you can't even trust to still be your friend if you're single, and…"

"Enough! You don't get to say that to me. You don't go to my school. You don't know my friends. And next year when you are off at college I am going to need my other friends." Alyssa stomped off towards her own front door.

Much later that night Alyssa heard a knock on her window. When she pulled the cord to raise the blinds she saw Brent's rather large frame crouched on the low roof. Oddly, the first thought to come to her mind was how much bigger he looked now than when they'd been ten and finding him outside her bedroom window was a daily occurrence.

"What?" Alyssa shouted through the glass just to emphasize that she was still angry with him.

"Open the window Lyssa."

"No."

"What did you mean?"

"Duh. I mean I'm not opening the window. Go home Brent."

"No, before. You said 'when *you* go away to college' why not when *we* go away?"

Alyssa opened the window so they could stop screaming, but she didn't let him in. Nope. She left Brent kneeling on the roof, in the cold even though it meant letting all that cold air in through the window. She was working on principal here.

"I just don't think I'm going to college that's all. I'm gonna get a job or something."

"You heard back from Penn State?"

"No. I didn't apply."

"We filled our applications out at the same time. Can I come in?" Brent shivered dramatically.

"No. You may not. I didn't send it."

"Lyssa, what is going on? It's due in like four weeks! Please tell me you are just proof reading the essay again."

"Can we not do this now? I'm freezing and I want to close the window."

"You're telling me. If I knew you were going to make me sit out here I would have at least put shoes on."

For the first time Alyssa noticed Brent's bare feet on the rough shingles. She moved aside and let him climb over the window sill. "I just don't think college is for me. I'm not sure what I am going to do yet, and I'm not good at anything like you are."

"Do your parents know? Whatever, that doesn't really matter. You are sending in the application Lyssa. You are good at lots of stuff, and how do you plan on deciding what to do with your life anyway? Can't you decide while you go to school?"

"It doesn't matter." Alyssa hadn't meant to tell him about the application. Her half-plan from the day she decided not to take the application to the post office was just to let him and everyone else think she didn't get in. Now it seemed to be less than half of a plan.

"Are you going to tell me what's going on?" Brent was staring at her. Alyssa realized she must have been quiet for awhile. Well it was her room and she had asked him to go home. So she could be quiet if she wanted to be quiet. "Lyssa?"

"I'm not smart. And that isn't me asking for pity or for praise. You know what my grades are like. And college is really hard. What's the point?"

"Who the crap told you weren't smart?!"

"SSSHHH!!!! You'll wake up my parents!"

"Is that where this is coming from?" Brent didn't have a lot of patience with Alyssa's mom and dad. They were less traditional then his parents—even if they were still happily married. They weren't bad parents they just weren't as involved as Ms. Carter was when they'd been growing up. But they were good parents—she had rules, and a curfew, and she was punished when she disregarded them.

"No. I told you. I just don't think I have the grades to get in that's all."

"You're grades are good enough. And you are smart. You just aren't studious. I can help you with your study habits if you would feel better."

"Can we talk about this later?" Alyssa was tired. The inside kind of tired. When you don't want to sleep, but you don't really want to be awake either.

Brent just looked at her for a few minutes. "I'm sorry about before Lyssa."

She just nodded. It wasn't the first fight they'd ever had and she wasn't really mad anymore. Besides she was starting to have a sneaking suspicion that he might have been right about some of it.

Brent climbed back to his own room. Alyssa laid down and didn't go to sleep for a long time.

Chapter Nine

How many bobbing buckets would she need? Alyssa was setting up her table with individual bobbing buckets. Because of the germs. The rest of her booth looked really good. A black table cloth and orange buckets for the bobbing went perfectly with the Halloween theme. And the wall behind her was covered with construction paper black cats, jack-o-lanterns, and ghosts. All the kids would also be receiving prizes in addition to their apples, so she had a big punch bowl filled with small plastic toys. The hospital had cleared out a big common room for them. All the other walls were also hung with Halloween decorations, and everywhere you looked there were games, activities, and arts and craft tables.

All the high school students were encouraged to wear costumes. Most of the girls were happy to dress up—a black tee shirt, a fuzzy eared headband, and a little creative use of her eyeliner transformed Alyssa into a cute kitty cat. Beth made a pretty angel. Her long blond hair looked extra shiny under the sparkly halo. Most of the boys wore their sports uniforms. So they ended up with a lot of football players, basketball players, and even a couple baseball players. Everything had come together really well and any minute the doors would be opened to the kids and their families. Alyssa should have been having fun except, well she wasn't.

"Alyssa! We need you." Tommy and Beth came rushing over to her.

"What's the matter?"

"The clown isn't coming."

"Oh. Well I do have the number for the agency." Alyssa reached for the day planner she'd been using to keep track of all the carnival information. As the most organized member of the Varsity Club she'd been elected event committee chairman. They'd spent a pretty chunk of change on the face painting clown.

"No. There isn't time. Couldn't you do it? We provided the special hypo allergenic face painting kit—now all we need is someone with a little talent." Tommy was holding out the face paint. "Brent says you're good."

"She's never lost a game of Pictionary." Brent walked up to them. She hadn't even known he was planning on coming.

"Brent!" He was standing there easily—as if they hadn't been fighting the last time they saw each other. He looked good too. Somewhere he'd found a Green Lantern tee shirt. His mom must have told him to wear a costume. The tee shirt was probably a left over from his comic book days, and it was a little tight now around his upper body.

"Come on!" Beth grabbed her arm and dragged her over the face painting booth. "Your cat face is perfect. And we can get anyone to do the bobbing thing." Brent trailed behind them.

"I can take photos of the kids after you do their faces. One of the nurses said she would make sure all the families got copies if we leave the memory card with her overnight." Tommy and Beth were gone and Brent and Alyssa were left standing there awkwardly staring at each other.

"Oh no!" Alyssa broke the silence when she groaned and dropped into a chair. "You're right. Things are getting weird!" She was completely serious, but for some reason Brent found her break down hilarious.

His laughter was contagious so she started laughing too. When they were both breathing normally again the weirdness was gone. She looked at him appraisingly. "You look good, but you know—the green lantern wore a mask." Alyssa pulled out a paint brush and shoved him into the other chair in front of her booth. When she was finished with him he had a green eye mask to go with his tee-shirt. This was just in time because the room was now filling up with kids ready for a good time.

For the next three hours everyone did have a good time. All the kids and even some of the parents visited the face painting booth. Brent's superhero mask was so popular that half the little boys demanded similar designs; a lot of the girls ended up as cats too. Alyssa was really enjoying herself. It should have been difficult to see how sick some of the children were, but all of them were smiling and laughing. It was actually more difficult, she decided, to feel bad for them. Instead she found herself admiring a girl pulling an IV stand decorated with pink sparkly stickers behind her. When a little boy asked her to paint a creepy spider web across his bald head Alyssa smiled and did just that. These kids didn't need her pity.

After packing up her booth and helping to mop up the mess around the bobbing for apples table Alyssa went looking for Brent. They'd spent most of the afternoon side by side, but she hadn't found a private moment with him to say thank you. He was lounging in a corner at one of the now empty craft tables with a couple of boys about 12 or 13 years old.

"No way, does Batman beat Superman! Superman can fly, has super strength, and he has laser vision! All Batman's got is a lame utility belt. No way!" One of the boys was arguing emphatically.

"Don't underestimate the utility belt, dude." Brent replied smiling. "Have you seen the stuff he pulls out of that thing?" Alyssa stood back for awhile listening to them. Brent looked more relaxed then she'd seen him in a long while.

"Once a loser, huh Carter?" Pete sneered when he walked up. Seeing the look on the older football player's face, the younger boys dropped their grins.

Alyssa grabbed the chair next to Brent and sat down. "Hey Brent. You never told me—which Green Lantern are you?"

Brent offered her a wide smile. "Hard to say—Hal Jordan was more of a badass, but I always liked Kyle Rayner. He makes me laugh."

"Yeah, Rayner's a good choice. I kinda dig John Stewart, but Rayner suits you better." Alyssa nodded.

Both boys and Pete dropped their jaws. "You know about the Green Lanterns?" One of the boys stammered out.

"Is there more than one?" Beth pulled up a chair to join the conversation. "I really wanted to see that movie. Ryan Reynolds is one of my favorite actors."

"Sure—the movie sucked though." Alyssa replied.

"I know!" Both boys exclaimed at once. After a discreet nod from Brent one of the boys launched into an explanation of the Green Lantern Corp and the Guardians of the Universe. Beth listened carefully and Pete was left, forgotten, standing next to them. He wandered off eventually, scowling as he went.

Alyssa dredged her memories to impress the boys with her comic book trivia. Beth joined in, sighting some of the cartoons she remembered. Beth thought that maybe Batman could beat Superman because didn't he have Robin and Batgirl to back him up? Alyssa sided with the boys out of sheer good-natured contrariness. Finally Beth and Alyssa stood up to leave. There was still work to do after all.

"Is she like your girlfriend? The cat?" Alyssa heard one of the boys ask and she slowed her steps to hear the rest.

"It's kind of complicated." Brent offered quietly.

"She's awesome—and so hot."

"Dude!" His friend slugged him in the shoulder and they both blushed.

"It's cool. She is." Brent sounded like he might be smiling.

That was all Alyssa could hear before someone handed her a box of decorations to carry out to her car. She couldn't help wondering which statement Brent had been agreeing with.

The next day was Friday—the day of the homecoming game. There would also be a parade featuring floats from all the school's clubs. Alyssa was dressed in her full cheerleading regalia for school. Her only concession to the weather was the leggings she wore beneath her short skirt.

"You gonna wear that all day? Like to classes?" Brent was carrying two plates from the stove to her kitchen table when she came downstairs. They looked like omelets. Her mouth watered.

"It's a tradition on game day." Alyssa replied. "What are you doing here?"

"Making breakfast. We need to talk."

"Oh." Alyssa had purposely slipped away from the hospital the night before, without talking privately with him. She'd decided not to ruin their perfect afternoon.

"I mailed your application."

That was so not what she was expecting him to say. "What?! How?"

"Your mom let me in yesterday afternoon, and I found it still in the envelope in your desk upstairs. So I mailed it on my way to the hospital." Brent shrugged and then shoveled several bites into his mouth.

Alyssa was speechless, so she ate too.

"I thought I'd drive you to school today. We can talk in the car." Brent finally spoke again after they'd rinsed their, now empty, plates. Taking her backpack from her, he headed out the door not waiting for an answer.

"When you get your acceptance letter—you can always turn it down if you decide you don't want to go." Brent started when they were on the road. "This way you have options."

"*If* I get in." She corrected him.

"Okay, *if* you get in." Brent chuckled at her. "If you decide to stay here—I'll still be you friend Lyssa. I feel ridiculous even saying that since it is a given, but...Well the other night you seemed like you needed to hear it." He waited for a response. Nothing came. "Things don't have to get weird—just so you know." This time Alyssa at least smiled. "What time is the parade thing?"

"5:15. I wasn't sure you were still planning on coming."

Brent rolled his eyes at her. "I said I would. Prince Charming will report for duty at 5:15 on the dot—as promised."

"Thanks." Alyssa moved to step out of the car.

Brent stopped her with a hand on her arm. "Have a good day, Chere." He grinned at her when she laughed out loud before heading towards the school doors.

Every year a lot of people turned out for the parade. It was a small town, and even the high school's homecoming game counted as big time entertainment. All the school organizations and clubs built floats. The cheerleaders had a very simple flat bed float decorated in blue and gold. Alyssa would be leading cheers from the center of the float. She didn't have time to find, or even look for, Brent before they lined up. The parade route circled two blocks, and ended up back in front of the school. It wasn't until after the parade floats were parked and the crowd was headed toward the football stadium that she found him. Actually he found her.

Alyssa and Beth were chatting with a couple of little girls dressed like cheerleaders. They were so adorable Alyssa and Beth couldn't resist lending them their blue and gold pompoms and teaching them a few simple cheers.

"You'll be cheering in a parade like this in no time at all." Alyssa was saying as she pulled out a little tube of glitter make up to make stars on each of their faces. Behind her she heard the familiar snapping of a camera shutter. Brent. "Enjoy the game guys!" Alyssa waved as the little girls danced off behind their parents.

Brent walked over to them quickly. "Hey, great job ladies!" He said as he swung an arm around Alyssa and the three of them headed over to the stadium together.

Most of the evening was a blur. Brent didn't take a stance at the railing behind the cheerleaders as he had the week before, but she saw him waving and clapping when they performed at half time. The squad got a break during the third quarter of the game. Brent was waiting for her with a cup of hot chocolate when she came off the field.

"Bring one for me?" Jennifer squeezed past Alyssa when she saw him.

"Sorry Jenny—I'm a one-hot-cocoa-man." Brent's long arm had no trouble reaching around her to pull Alyssa out of the crowd. "Your parents are here. They brought your Pop too." Brent leaned over to whisper in her ear.

"They never come to this stuff!" Alyssa panicked. Things would get real weird real quick if her mom and dad saw Brent's boyfriend routine.

"I know. I think Pop called them—he wanted to come."

"What are we going to do? Maybe we could hide? We only have to avoid them for fifteen minutes." She looked over at Brent when he didn't answer. He was staring straight ahead and mumbling something so low she could only see his lips moving. "What are you saying?"

"I was counting to ten." Brent sighed his now familiar sigh. "You really want to avoid Pop? For fifteen *football* minutes?"

"I don't *want* to, but do you want to explain all the handholding?" She held up their intertwined fingers for emphasis.

"Let's get some food. We can't hold hands while we eat." Brent still wasn't looking at her, but at least he'd stopped sighing. And the food thing was brilliant. For a guy who wasn't overly fond of subterfuge he sure thought fast on his feet.

Carrying a tray laden with nachos and popcorn, they joined her family in the bleachers. "Good game tonight." Pop said after he'd hugged her hello. "That Edser kid's pretty good." Brent choked on a popcorn kernel. A few minutes fluttered by. They talked about the game, and Alyssa's mom complimented the squad's half time show.

"Got room for one more?" Beth asked from the aisle, and Alyssa made her family scoot down along the bench seat. "Nice to meet you." Beth said after introductions had been made. They all sat together snacking and enjoying the game until it was time for Beth and Alyssa to rejoin the squad. As far as Alyssa could tell no one suspected anything. Her parents and Pop were still in the dark about her fake relationship, and Beth didn't seem to think anything was off either. By the end of the night Alyssa was exhausted.

"You look amazing." Beth was fastening Alyssa's necklace for her. It was the finishing touch. Beth had been at Alyssa's house since the early afternoon. Now, they were almost ready for the limo and the boys to pick them up. Looking in her full length mirror Alyssa silently agreed with her friend. The warm coffee color of her dress made her skin look creamier, and her hair look glossier. Her favorite part was the beaded bodice that brought subtle attention to her push-up-bra-enhanced cleavage. Beth looked good too. She'd opted for a high collared, but backless gown in sapphire blue.

Her own blue eyes popped more than usual because of the color. And her hair was swept back off her face in a neat French knot, leaving her neck seductively bare.

"You look pretty amazing yourself. Tommy's going to swallow his tongue." The girls shared a giggle.

"That's kind of the idea. He's so amazing. Sometimes when I see him walking down the hall at school I can actually feel the butterflies in my stomach! I've never felt like this about anyone. And he's so sweet too— not at all pushy you know?"

"Actually most of the guys I've dated have been the pushy type."

Beth's face filled with concern. "Really? Brent seems so laid back, but I can see that about Pete."

Oops. She was supposed to be dating Brent, right. "Oh, not Brent. He would never push." She hurried to correct herself and clear her friend's name.

"Well I'm glad. But you've known each other for ages, right? So I bet it was pretty natural…" Beth seemed to read the discomfort in Alyssa's face because she let the subject drop.

"Alyssa! The boys are here!" Her dad was yelling up the stairs to them. Alyssa was never happier to end a conversation in her life.

At the bottom of the stairs Alyssa was surprised to find Brent waiting with Tommy. She was sure she'd told him to go right to the limo.

"That's a beautiful dress, Lyssa." He murmured as he held out a corsage box. He did look incredible. As much as Alyssa loathed agreeing with Jennifer—he did look *yummy* in a suit.

"Thanks. You clean up pretty good yourself Carter." Alyssa joked to cover up the butterfly feeling in her stomach. Damn Beth for planting these ridiculous thoughts in her head. Brent did not give her butterflies. He didn't!

"This is so nice, you two going to the dance together." Alyssa's dad started to talk.

"We gotta go dad! Bye!" Alyssa pulled the others out the front door before her father could blow their cover.

"Why'd you come inside?" She whispered fiercely to Brent as they made their way towards the limo sitting at the curb.

"Must be the gentleman in me." Brent replied wryly. "Don't worry those two can't see anything but each other." He gestured to where Tommy and Beth were walking arm in arm in front of them.

Alyssa's house was the limo driver's last stop and climbing in was a problem. It was a very tight fit indeed. Of course when they'd originally ordered the car they hadn't counted on Lisa or Brent. Alyssa was very glad for the dim lights inside because she was suddenly reminded of her bold statement to Jennifer of how she would solve the space issue. And she was very sure that sitting in Brent's lap would be a bad way to discourage her traitorous butterfly-filled stomach. Lucky for her she was spared that experience when at the other end of the long bench seat Pete dragged a giggling Lisa into his lap. The two of them groping five feet away from her probably should have bothered her, but she was too busy being bothered in an entirely different way by the smell of Brent's cologne, and the warmth of his body against hers. Since when did Brent wear cologne?

At the school and out of the limo, fresh air helped calm Alyssa down. Dim lights and slightly cheesy decorations transformed the gym. Tables lined three of the walls and a DJ was set up on the fourth wall. The room was crowded to capacity and every time Alyssa turned around she was saying hello and complimenting someone's dress or suit. Alyssa and Brent settled themselves at a table next to Beth and Tommy. As soon as they sat down Jenn and Jeff claimed the last remaining chairs. To Alyssa's dismay Jenn ended up on the other side of Brent, and Jeff wasn't paying enough attention to mind at all.

To Brent's credit he ignored all of Jenn's pointed advances and he was very attentive to Alyssa. They danced to all her favorite songs—he even did the chicken dance which broke Alyssa into a fit of laughter so violent they had to leave the dance floor in search of the punch bowl. Dancing with Brent was just as disconcerting as sitting next to him in that crowded limo. Even after he'd discarded his jacket and tie, and looked more like his usual self, she found her heart leaping strangely when he pulled her close for the slow songs.

At some point during the evening Alyssa was able to forget that this was a fake reputation-saving-date and she just started having fun. Tommy, as it turns out, was a big hockey fan. And even though he was a Penguins fan Alyssa still enjoyed his company. Before she'd gotten closer to Beth she hadn't noticed Tommy very much.

"Are you guys gonna talk hockey all night?" Beth was laughing, but Alyssa could tell she was also bored.

"Sorry. I guess I got carried away. I can't believe you've never been to a game before. We should go sometime."

Beth beamed. "Yay, a double date! That does sound fun."

Alyssa worked very hard not to look at Brent. She hadn't meant to set up another date where he would be obligated to play prince charming again. It just slipped out.

"It does." Tommy was saying. "I guess my reputation can handle sitting next to a couple of Flyers fans."

"Come on, Chere. I like this song." Brent stood up and led Alyssa to the dance floor.

Crap. She was in trouble again. And she'd been having such a good time too. It was her own fault really. She knew where Brent stood on the whole fake boyfriend thing. "I'm so sorry Brent." She said when he'd settled her against him.

"Hmm?" He looked down at her.

"About the game thing. I'll get out of it later."

"We can go to a game, Lyssa. We go to games together all the time. And Beth and Tommy are cool, it'll be fun."

Alyssa was confused. "Why are we dancing then? I mean, if you didn't drag me out on the dance floor to yell at me?"

Brent sighed. Alyssa barely noticed the sighing anymore. "We're at a dance. I like this song. So I asked you to dance with me. Not everything has five lines of subtext attached to it. And I hardly dragged you—what am I, Captain Caveman?"

Alyssa stepped a little closer. It was so easy to pretend this was a real date. Thinking about pretending her pretend date wasn't pretending gave her a head ache. So for a moment she let herself stop thinking. Brent wasn't that much taller than her when she wore heels. She was able to tilt her head upward and bring her face very close to his.

"Can I cut in?" Pete appeared beside them. He was slurring his words together.

"No." Brent spun Alyssa around turning his back to him.

"I was asking her." Pete reached out to grab Alyssa's wrist, but he was obviously drunk, and he stumbled forward missing her completely. Turning, he glared at her "You never danced with me that way." He was thankfully speaking at a normal volume, but Alyssa was still mortified. When he started to reach for her again Brent's hand closed around his bicep.

"Let's take a walk Edser." He turned to Alyssa. "I'll be right back, Lyssa." She hesitated. "I'm just gonna call him a cab, go sit with Tommy and Beth." Turning, he walked Pete towards the exit.

Alyssa was too shocked to do anything else, so she sat down with Beth as he'd instructed. Out of the corner of one eye she saw Lisa Thompson hurrying to follow them.

"What's that all about?" Beth asked.

"Oh, I guess Pete's been drinking. Brent is going to call him a cab."

Jennifer was stretching her neck trying to see out the exit doors. This wasn't possible because the lights were dimmed for the dance, but it was clear Jenn was sorry that she might be missing a news worthy scene. "I do hope he gets out of here before a teacher sees him. That would be the end of our football season." Everyone at the table glared at her, and she had the grace to blush slightly. "Well it must be nice to have such a strong man around to defend your honor." Alyssa ignored her, but privately she thought that yes, it was nice.

Brent returned to the table. "Pete and Lisa had to leave early." Was all he said. Alyssa admired him so much. Always cool and collected in any situation. He really was very nice to have around. The rest of the evening went by pleasantly, if unremarkably. At one point Jennifer did try and get Brent to dance with her, but he refused her politely.

They'd been the last stop on the way to the dance, so at the end of the evening they were the first to be let out. "Night guys!" Alyssa called over her shoulder as Brent walked her to the front door.

Brent's tall large body was very close to her as she put her key in the lock. Alyssa wondered if he noticed her hand shaking. Really—when had he started to wear cologne?

"Invite me in." He whispered into her ear.

"Okay sure." Was her voice squeaking? She suddenly felt very sure that their relationship was about to experience a big change.

He followed her inside and once the door was shut Alyssa turned around slowly to face him. He wasn't there!

Brent was in the kitchen pouring himself a glass of milk. "You guys need to keep more junk food around. All that dancing makes a guy crave carbs." He said lightly when she walked in.

"What are you doing?"

"Oh." He looked a little confused and then he reached into the cabinet again. "Did you want a glass?"

"No. I meant, well…you wanted me to invite you in so you could insult our pantry?"

"Not the actual pantry—just its contents." He grinned. "Your friends were watching. They would have at least expected a kiss goodnight at the door." He clarified for her.

Right. Pretend boyfriend. Pretend date. What was wrong with her anyway? It wasn't like she'd wanted that kiss goodnight. Man, they had to end this fake boyfriend thing soon. Her emotions couldn't take it anymore.

"Oh." That was it. That was all she could think to say. So she walked around him, opened a cabinet, and pulled out a box of lucky charms.

"Sweet." Brent grabbed the box from her. "Go change. I'll put a DVD in." And he walked carelessly into her family room. Just as he'd done a thousand times before. She really had to get a hold of herself.

When she was changed, she came back downstairs to find Brent spread out on her couch; his feet propped up, one hand reaching into the cereal box, and watching the opening scenes of the first Harry Potter movie. He knew she preferred Richard Harris to Michael Gambon's

Dumbledore. The sight was so familiar. Just Brent hanging out, watching a movie. Alyssa happily joined him on the couch.

"I had a good time tonight Lyssa. Mostly."

"Mostly?"

"Yeah, well you pretty much go to school in a John Hughes movie. But I like Tommy and Beth. And you were there—I like you."

"Thanks." She snorted a little. "I like you too."

"Hillfield's homecoming is next week. If you want we could go."

Did he sound nervous? No. Brent never sounded nervous. "Like a date?"

"I don't know, Lyssa. I just thought you might want to go. And I can hardly take someone else. Do we have to make a big deal out of it?"

"No. I mean yes—we should go." Alyssa recovered quickly. Of course it wasn't a real date. "I'll get Beth to go dress shopping with me."

"What's wrong with the brown dress? I liked it."

"Coffee. It's not *brown*. And you don't wear dresses like that twice."

"Girls are dumb."

"Yeah well—at least we don't have cooties." Alyssa stole the Lucky Charms box from him.

Chapter Ten

It was Wednesday before Beth was free to go to the mall with Alyssa. That was cutting it a little close, but she'd been regretting bailing on Beth for dress shopping a few weeks before. And shopping alone didn't sound like much fun. "I like the red one." Beth was saying as she passed several choices over the top of a dressing room door. "Red would look good with your hair."

"I was thinking green." Alyssa mumbled from inside. Jenn's dress had been a perfect emerald green satin. Exactly the shade of Brent's eyes.

"There's a green one in this pile. But I don't think you should limit yourself to one color just because of what Jenn said."

Stupid Jennifer. "I'm not. I just like green that's all." She opened the door wearing a floor length moss green shift with a filmy overskirt.

"Very nice. Better than Jenn's for sure."

"I hardly remember Jenn's dress." Alyssa said aloud, while inside she loudly and emphatically agreed that this dress was way better than Jenn's. "This is the one."

"Wow. I've never bought a dress in under 30 minutes before." Beth started hanging the discarded options on the dressing room rack. "It does seem like it was made for you though. Want to get some dinner as long as we're out?"

"Chinese?"

Beth wrinkled up her face. "I'd rather anything else. There's a Mexican place in the food court that's pretty good."

Enchiladas in hand, they found a table in the food court. "Can I ask you a question?" Beth asked after a moment.

Alyssa nodded.

"What's really the deal with you and Brent?"

Alyssa started choking. "Sorry, umm spicy." She said after sucking down half her soda. "What did you mean?"

"Look if it's none of my business that's fine. I just thought…well he only *just* asked you to his homecoming? Your dad was kinda surprised he was going with you last weekend, and sometimes you seem to forget you even have a boyfriend." Beth shook her head. "Just so you know— I think Pete's a jerk. So do half the kids at our school. And only Jenn thinks she's important. Mostly people ignore her."

Busted. Beth was a lot more perceptive than she'd given her credit for. "Brent and I—" What could she say? Lying was getting to be so exhausting and confusing. "We are still figuring things out, I guess." She finished a little lamely. It was basically true.

Beth seemed to accept that—even if it was lame. "Well your dress is perfect. Make sure to take pictures okay?"

The rest of the meal conversation was dedicated to more interesting and superficial topics. Such as Tommy's crazy obsession with his car:

"Really! He made me take off my shoes before getting in last week!"

And the rumor that their chemistry teacher was actually a member of witness protection. "It would totally explain why he needs to check his teacher edition every ten seconds. It's the blind leading the blind in that class." This was from Alyssa but Beth was nodding in agreement.

And of course about Lisa Thompson's sudden disinterest in Pete. "I guess she wasn't too happy about him drooling all over you at the dance"

"I don't think I'd say drooling. He was just drunk. I am glad he left quietly though. Wasn't it smooth the way Brent just handled things?"

Beth looked like she was trying not to smile. "It was. Very Smooth."

When Brent picked her up on Saturday night there were fewer butterflies. This was because she'd been preparing herself all day for the sight of him in formal wear.

"I'm glad you bought a new dress. It's nice." Brent commented when they found a table in the Hillfield gym. This was the first time Alyssa'd been to the exclusive private school. She wasn't sure why, but the fact that this room largely resembled her own school's gym only with different a different color scheme really surprised her.

"Thanks."

They'd driven over in Brent's car, but a group of his friends were saving them seats when they arrived. James, Liz, Matt, Ella, Patrick, and what was his date's name? Sandy maybe? She would have to wait for someone else to speak to her and try to catch her name then.

"We've heard a lot about you Lyssa." Liz spoke up when Brent was off getting them drinks.

"All good I hope." Alyssa offered a shy smile. This was a new smile for her because she wasn't usually a shy person. But what had they heard about her?

"Oh, yeah." James put in. "Brent says you throw a mean long ball."

"And that you know everything worth knowing about hockey and every other sport worth watching." Patrick added.

"And that's good?" Alyssa's real smile came out.

"Yes!" All three guys said at once.

"He also told us you organized a charity carnival for the hospital." Liz shot her date a pointed look. "And that you're something of a math whiz."

"She carried my ass through Trig last year." Brent returned to the table with a couple of sodas.

"You were doing fine. I just double checked his homework every now and then." Alyssa blushed. It was nice, she thought, that Brent was talking her up to his friends. Usually when someone complimented her it was on cheering, or on her appearance. This was way better.

"Okay so who's your favorite hockey player?" Patrick asked her.

"Current player or overall?"

Patrick grinned. "Overall"

"Bobby Clarke. Hands down. Loyalty is important to me—he spent the most seasons as a Flyer. Plus he was the youngest ever NHL captain in 1972, until Schoenfeld in 74."

The boys looked stunned and a little impressed. Actually a few of their dates looked impressed too.

"Schoenfeld didn't play for the Flyers." Patrick accused lightly.

"Never said he did. He was with Buffalo." Alyssa chirped happily.

"Alright, alright! My date isn't a party trick." Brent was chuckling as he stood up. "Dance with me Lyssa."

He tucked her just under his chin and settled into a slow swaying dance step. "I like your friends." Alyssa was talking against her shoulder.

"They like you too. It's funny isn't it?"

"What? That your friends like me?" Alyssa pulled back to look him in the eye.

Brent laughed and spun her around. "No. That you're just meeting them and that I never knew Beth or Tommy before…all this."

"You've known Beth and Tommy since we were all kids."

"You know what I mean, Lyssa."

"Yeah, I guess I do."

They had a great time. Dancing, joking, sharing stories. It was hands down her best date ever. Alyssa was happy to play 20 questions with all of Brent's friends. They included her like she'd known them for years. That was a big perk of being Brent's best friend. He had this way of making himself a part of the crowd and towing her along with him. He was never the center of a party—that would have been too much pressure. But he was always there, moving with the action.

At the end of the night Brent and Alyssa were some of the last to leave. Even then Alyssa was reluctant. Here, away from the labels and pressures of the past few weeks, she felt happier and more relaxed than… well than ever. And those butterflies in her stomach? They weren't all bad; she was kind of getting used to them.

In the car on their way home they sang along with the radio at the top of their lungs. Alyssa thought they did *Still Rock and Roll* better than Billy Joel. Wheezer's *Buddy Holly* was more difficult, but really did anyone know all those lyrics? She was out of breath when they pulled into his driveway.

"This was fun, Brent. I'm glad you asked me."

"Well I guess that's better than *I appreciated it*." They both laughed at the memory of their first fake date. The laughter drifted off into silence. Leaving the air between them charged with light tension. There was a whole 'new territory' feeling about this night. Alyssa wasn't totally sure she liked that—but neither did she want it to end.

"Are you going to invite me in?" Alyssa asked after a few moments of quiet.

"I'm still thinking about it." Brent's whisper was close to her, and Alyssa realized they'd been leaning toward each other. In the dark of the parked car she couldn't read the expression on his face. But excitement was breaking out in her blood stream, and her body hummed at the idea of kissing him.

Kissing Brent! Whoa! Alyssa straightened up. She didn't want to kiss Brent. Brent was her buddy. They played Mario Cart and helped each other with their homework. "I think I'm tired. I'll call you tomorrow." She bolted out of the car and down the sidewalk toward her house.

"Lyssa! Lyssa, wait!" She could hear him behind her but she wasn't stopping for anything.

Brent called her cell phone three times before she turned it off. She left it off all weekend. Even though that meant going to Pop's by herself, and having to play chess. Her mind was running a mile a minute. Brent had almost kissed her. She was pretty sure anyway that he'd been going to kiss her. In the daylight and out of her fancy dress it was hard to be sure exactly what happened. Probably she could ask Brent. Right. Like that was gonna happen.

The strangest part was that she couldn't even decide if she wanted him to kiss her. At the time—sure she'd wanted it. But kissing Brent would change everything. And she wasn't very sure she wanted things to change. Besides, until that moment Alyssa had been pretty well convinced that Brent wasn't attracted to her. He'd never said anything anyway. It must be all this fake dating—they were buying into their own hype.

On Monday Alyssa left for school really early. Just in case Brent tried another breakfast ambush. At some point she was going to have to face him, this was not that time. Before she talked to Brent she needed to get her head on straight. First order of business—put the kibosh on the boyfriend charade. Of course how does one go about stopping a rumor? Lucky for her Jennifer's incessant prying finally came in handy.

At lunch, when Alyssa settled into her seat next to Beth at the cheerleader's table, Jennifer, as always, began digging for gossip. This time she got some.

"So what were you and Brent up to over the weekend?" Jenn asked even before her butt was completely in the chair.

"Actually. Brent and I decided we weren't working out. We are going to cool things off, go back to being friends." Alyssa hoped she sounded nonchalant, but just in case she took two big bites of her taco salad to cover any betraying facial expressions.

"That must be hard." Jennifer didn't bother trying to cover up her grin. "Was he seeing someone else? A girl at Hillfield I'll bet."

"What!? No." Alyssa was horrified. She didn't want them to think badly of him. What had she gotten him into?

"Brent would never do that." Beth piped up, but she shot a questioning look at Alyssa. "You don't have to explain to us—it isn't *our* business." She continued staring pointedly at Jennifer.

"No, it's okay. I just don't think we were meant to be more than friends I guess. Brent is a great guy."

"Oh now I get it." Jenn started again, completely disregarding Beth's death stare. "This is about Pete. Now that he's available again, you just drop poor Brent. That's just awful of you. He loved you for all those years, and you were just using him? Poor Brent." Jenn was shaking her head. "He could probably use a friend to talk to right about now." The grin was back.

Alyssa would have been livid with Jennifer, accept that at the moment it was very clear to her that Jenn actually was just as sad and pathetic as Brent had claimed, and not really worth being angry at. Besides in a roundabout way she was kind of right. Alyssa had used Brent. Even if she was reasonably sure he hadn't been pining for her. After all he'd gone out of his way the past three weeks to avoid kissing her, and he never paid her any romantic compliments. She'd actually come right out and asked him several times if he thought she was pretty, and he always found a way to avoid answering. Everyone knew that was just a diplomatic way of saying *no, not really*. Then again…he *had* almost kissed her in the car. Crap. She was going to have to have that conversation sooner than she'd planned.

"Alyssa? Are you paying attention?" Beth was waving her open hand in front of Alyssa's eyes.

"No, I'm sorry what were you saying?"

"Nothing very important. Do you want to go someplace and talk? Someplace private?" She shot another less than subtle look at Jenn.

"No. I'm fine really. Just tired."

Beth nodded. She looked like she wanted to say something else but instead she went back to her own taco salad.

Chapter Eleven

That night Alyssa sat in her room from the moment she'd finished dinner until the moment she saw the light come on next door. Every five or so minutes she'd just about get up the nerve to call him, but she always chickened out before hitting *send*. With the light on she knew he must be home, so there wasn't going to be anymore avoidance.

Alyssa crawled out of her window, and tapped lightly on his. He answered immediately.

"Should I make you sit on the roof all night?" He joked lightly.

"You probably could. I think there is a distinct possibility that I deserve it."

Brent pulled a face. "Get in here Lyssa."

Alyssa climbed in. Normally she would make herself comfortable—maybe plop down on the floor, or even lounge across his bed. Now she just stood awkwardly shifting her weight from side to side. "We broke up." She finally managed.

"I thought we might have." Brent was sitting in his desk chair, watching her with those super intense eyes of his. "Care to tell me why?"

"You're supposed to be happy. You hated being my boyfriend. And anyway things were getting a little confused."

"Okay."

That was it? Two days of ignoring his phone calls. The entire school was mad at her for leading him on and then breaking his heart. Well maybe not the whole school, but some of them. He was just going to sit there and stare at her? No. Way. "That's it? That's all you have to say?"

"What am I supposed to say, Lyssa?"

"I don't know! Something! How did you know we broke up? I mean that I told people…whatever—how did you know?"

"Jenny wants to help me work through my broken heart." He replied sarcastically. "What *did* you tell people?"

"I tried to keep it simple, but you know how she is. Now everyone hates me for leading you on, since you've been pining for me since we were ten."

Brent laughed. Was her imagination or did he laugh at her a lot lately? Of course laughing was better than some of the other scenarios she'd been picturing. Maybe this would be the end of it and they'd be Alyssa and Brent again. Just like before.

"That does clear up some of her phone call. Are we going to talk about Saturday night?" He leaned back in his chair slightly, his eyes unblinking.

Damn. Maybe she wasn't going to get off that easily. "If you want to." He just tilted his head at her. Clearly he'd been expecting a little more from her. "Was it real? The date I mean, was it a real date?"

"Do you want it to be?"

"Brent! Now is not the time to play therapist with me. Have I been leading you on?!?"

"What?" Brent looked surprised.

"Well I didn't think so—I mean I know you aren't interested in me that way, but Jenn and Sue seemed so sure…"

"How do you know that?" He might as well have been asking after the weather forecast. His tone of voice gave nothing away.

Stressful tears started pricking at Alyssa's eyelids. Stupid girl hormones! She fought them off. "Well you don't…I mean it's fine, but you're not attracted to me so…" He raised his eyebrows at her. "I ask you all the time. You never say I'm pretty. But that's okay." Alyssa rushed on.

"Come on Lyssa! You own a mirror, you know you're gorgeous." Brent sighed at her. She had honestly thought that relieving him of fake boyfriend duties would get her out of sighing range. "I didn't think you needed to hear that from me. What was I supposed to say? It would have been weird if I mentioned it every time you took my breath away just by walking into a room. But okay. Yeah, I'm attracted to you."

"Oh man!" Alyssa crumpled to the floor.

"See? I told you it would be weird." Brent sounded slightly amused. "I don't suppose you have anything you want to say to me?"

"Of course—I'm sorry. I didn't mean to lead you on. I swear I had no idea how you felt."

"What?" Brent jerked his gaze to hers; his eyes were—what? Maybe angry? "Lyssa I haven't been…what did you call it?… *pining* for you since we were ten. Is that why you're here? To apologize for breaking my heart?"

"No. Maybe. I didn't?" Alyssa looked up at him. "I don't know why I'm here Brent. I just want things to be normal for us again. What are the chances of us just pretending the last month never happened?"

"I think we've done enough pretending lately. Maybe you should just go, Lyssa. You let me know when you're ready to talk for real."

"That is completely unfair Brent! I *am* here. We *are* talking. Actually mostly I am talking and you get to sit there and sigh and roll your eyes at me a whole lot. You know what? You're right, I am gonna go. I think maybe we could use a bit of a break." Alyssa scrambled out his window, and back into hers. She stayed awake most of the night waiting for him to come tapping at her window—but he didn't.

On Tuesday she left for school late. This time she was hoping for a breakfast ambush—she didn't get one. Whatever. She didn't need all those extra calories anyway. Brent put too much cheese in his omelets. At school she wandered around in her own world. By the end of the day Beth had taken to calling her *zombie girl*.

"You gonna tell me what brought the zombie on?" She asked when practice was over and they were headed for the parking lot. "Did you fight with Brent?"

"I told you yesterday that we broke up."

"Yeah, you did. I just didn't buy it until today. You are pretty out of it."

Alyssa considered lying, but she was tired of lying. Especially to Beth. "Brent and I did have a fight. At least I think we did. We were never really dating at all you know. Jenn assumed, and I just didn't want people talking after that mess with Pete."

"I thought it might be something like that. But you seemed happy together."

"He's my best friend. We are always happy together. At least we were. He really hates gossip; he only went along with it because I basically begged him."

"So, why the fight?"

"Who knows. Things just got weird. I kind of accused him of being in love with me."

"And?"

"And—he's not."

"Oh. Awkward…" Beth's eyes went all sympathetic.

Alyssa was so tired of dealing with this whole issue. "Do you want to do something? Get a smoothie at the mall maybe?"

Beth was very easy to get along with. She happily agreed and they spent the remainder of the afternoon on light topics that didn't make Alyssa's head (or heart) ache.

On Friday she got her Shakespeare paper back in English class. It was her first A in that class all year. Of course there was no way she'd have done so well if she hadn't reworked the entire thing according to Brent's comments. Twice she pulled out her phone to text him a thank you. He would be glad for her. At least he would have been if they were talking to each other—but they weren't. Apparently they were on a break. And it was her stupid idea. The Shakespeare paper ended up in the bottom of her back pack.

Saturday was the last Cheer meet of the season. All the girls went to a party at Jennifer's house to celebrate. A couple of weeks ago a party at Jenn's house would have been pretty low on her list of things she'd like to do. We are talking lower than swimming with leeches. Now she was looking forward to hanging out with Beth—besides her other option for the weekend was to stay home alone not calling Brent.

"It's kind of too bad we didn't do a little better. It would have been nice to make it to the championships at least once before we graduated." Beth was saying. She and Alyssa were curled up on the floor playing with the Pastings' ancient German Sheppard. Some Cheer teams went on to compete through the winter. They weren't ranked well enough to compete at a higher level.

"I guess. But I like having time off between seasons." Alyssa wasn't bothered by their low standings. Now that she thought about it cheering was one of the only things Alyssa didn't feel competitive about. Usually she relished her open schedule during the holidays. Of course historically speaking she'd filled those open weekends with Brent. Thanksgiving was still two weeks away—surely by then Brent would be speaking to her again. Wouldn't he?

"I can't tomorrow, my Hillfield man wants to go to a movie." Jenn drew out the word Hillfield as if she was saying *sex god*.

Alyssa's whole body spun around involuntarily. Jenn was walking past them with Sue. Brent and Jenn were going to a movie? That was just terrific. Great even. He could do whatever he wanted; he wasn't her pretend boyfriend anymore anyway. Of course this meant she'd be visiting Pop alone again. Poor Pop would be subjected to her subpar chess tactics. Maybe Brent didn't care about that though.

"Hey—you have to take everything she says with a grain of salt. You know that." Alyssa forced herself to focus on Beth's voice.

"It's fine. I told you we aren't together. I'm gonna go home. I'll see you on Monday."

Alyssa fled to her car.

Thanksgiving arrived, and Brent still didn't call. Alyssa hated mashing the potatoes; usually Brent did that part for her. Most years he would have been at the Maddow's all morning. Watching the parade on TV, helping in the kitchen, and tossing a football in the yard. He would have gone home around 1:00 when his grandparents arrived. So it was hardly as though her holiday was ruined. Pop was happy to watch the parade with her, and chess was nearly as much fun as playing catch—anyway it was warmer. During dinner Alyssa kept glancing out the window to see if any extra cars were at the Carter's. Like maybe Jennifer's silver Jetta. She didn't see it, but that didn't make her feel any better.

In school Alyssa tried to be her usual cheerful self. It wasn't fair that Brent could ruin school days for her as well as weekends. They went to different schools—it wasn't like she'd lost something. Of course her usual cheerful self was getting harder and harder to pull off. Actually she was pretty sure that no one was buying it. During lunch Jennifer was constantly hinting at her big evening plans—trying to bait Alyssa into asking her what they were. Alyssa started taking her lunch to the library. She needed the study time.

After school Alyssa was too busy to notice if Brent's car was in the drive or not. Her Mom and Dad were going to regret all their eating out when their blood pressures were through the roof. So she started going to the market, and she took charge of dinners. Her pasta was never as good as Brent's, but she made a fabulous turkey pot pie and her chicken tacos were to die for. As it turned out not having Brent around all the time wasn't so bad after all. Her grades shot up—probably because he wasn't always there distracting her while she tried to study. And she didn't have nearly as many sleepy mornings now that he wasn't keeping her up until all hours playing video games. For the first time in memory all of her Christmas shopping was done early.

Sometime in December, remembering actual dates had become less important to Alyssa lately, Beth was waiting to ambush her outside her last class of the day. They sly smile on her face made Alyssa nervous even before she noticed the small thin box covered in Santa Claus faces in her outstretched hand. "Christmas isn't for, umm…8—no 9 days yet." She objected thinking of the not yet wrapped Rihanna CD she'd chosen for Beth—still at home in her bedroom.

"I know. But this is a time sensitive gift." Beth shook the box at her with impatience.

Opening the gift, Alyssa lifted one of several tickets from the layer of tissue paper. "Billy Joel?"

Beth grinned. "I know you are a fan. The concert's this weekend… so time sensitive."

"I am. A fan I mean. There are four tickets here." Alyssa was pleased. Billy Joel was a favorite of hers. She didn't remember telling Beth that. She was such a good friend.

"Well Tommy and I are going too, and his cousin, Spencer, is a big Billy Joel fan—so he makes four."

Alyssa nodded. "Wow this is great thanks!"

"Actually I'm kind of excited too. I looked him up—he did all the music for *movin out*. I loved that show"

"I know." Alyssa fought a memory of Ms. Carter taking her and Brent to see the Broadway production a few years before.

Chapter Twelve

Beth and company picked her up Saturday afternoon. "Alyssa, Spencer, Spencer, Alyssa." Beth was saying when she reached Tommy's car in the driveway. "Spencer is at Penn State. Didn't you say you applied there?"

"Yeah, I guess so. Do you like it there?

"It's alright. School is still school though." Spencer was very nice looking. A little taller than she was, with short dark hair bright twinkling eyes, he'd been leaned against the passenger side of Tommy's car and now was holding the door open for her.

"Thanks." She slid into the back seat.

"Alyssa is a big hockey fan." Beth continued when she and Spencer had settled into their seats and they were headed towards the arena.

"But she's a Flyers fan." Tommy put in.

"So definitely not the perfect woman, huh?" Spencer joked. "We are strictly Pittsburg fans in our family. Shame too—you being so pretty and all."

Hockey was something Alyssa could talk about all night long. And she almost did. Beth didn't even seem to mind that she was being excluded from the conversation. It was a nice idea, Alyssa thought, for Beth to have invited Spencer. This way no one felt like a third wheel.

The show was terrific. Their seats more or less qualified as nose bleeds, but it was still a lot of fun. She sang along with every song, and they all danced in the isles during *uptown girl*.

"I had no idea I would know so many songs!" Beth exclaimed after the concert. They'd ended up in a corner booth of a campy old diner on the highway ordering pie and milkshakes.

"I told you he was famous—my mom listens to his stuff all the time." Tommy teased her. "C'mon let's check out the claw machine." He tugged Beth out of the booth and off into the small arcade area next to the hostess station.

"So. Good concert huh?" Spencer asked when they were alone.

"Yeah. I've never seen him live before—I think he hit all my favorites. How about yours? What's your favorite Billy Joel song?"

"Oh, well I like *uptown girls* I guess. This isn't my usual style."

"Oh. Beth said you were a fan. That's why she invited you." He just looked at her. "Oh. My. God. They set us up! This is supposed to be a *date*."

Spencer's eyes crinkled up a little and he nodded slowly at her. "I think that's pretty obvious."

"You knew?"

"Umm, yeah. Music. Food. Date. Anyway I broke up with my high school girl friend over the summer and I think Tommy's been feeling bad for me. Happy couples are always trying to put together more happy couples." Spencer clearly thought she was insane for taking so long to figure it out.

"I'm sorry. I wasn't thinking...along those lines."

"It's fine. Now that you know—what do you think?"

"About being on a date with you?" Panicked, sad, and a little sick to my stomach Alyssa answered to herself. "I'm sorry. I'm just not in a dating place right now. Sorry."

Spencer was looking at her strangely. "You don't need to apologize three times. You've hardly broken my heart."

"It seems I'm *not* breaking a lot of hearts lately."

Alyssa was saved from the embarrassment of having spoken out loud by the return of Tommy and Beth. At the end of the night Alyssa was very glad to be going home. Being on a non–double-date was pretty awkward once you actually knew it was a non–double-date.

Chapter Thirteen

Christmas came and went. Alyssa was grateful for the week off of school. She was tired—she could probably use the rest. Lately she could barely seem to find the energy to make it to school on time. Every year since they were 12 Brent left town to spend the holidays with his dad. Last year they'd gone skiing in Vermont. It was dumb to miss his company during a time of year she was use to being alone anyway. Of course last year she'd gotten beautiful postcards, funny emails, and whatever—she didn't miss him *that* much.

It was a good holiday even without a call from her best friend. Alyssa determinedly disregarded the still wrapped gift under the tree addressed to Brent. Normally he would have been over a few days earlier to exchange gifts before he left for his dad's. This year the super light weight aluminum collapsible tripod wrapped in shiny green paper laughed at her from beneath the tree. He hadn't come. Whatever, she'd bought the thing weeks ago anyway. Before the stupid break.

Pop loved the baseball game she'd bought him for his Wii. She stayed later than usual that evening after bringing Pop home just to try it out with him. She won. It was way more fun than chess. "So does this mean I am off the hook for Sunday chess games now? I'll play as much baseball as you want." Alyssa goaded her grandfather a little. He liked it that way.

"We'll see about that, girl. These TV games take a little practice. I never used to be good at the bowling one either. Did Steven tell you I bowled a perfect game last week?"

"No. That's great Pop."

"Yeah he bowls with me on Tuesdays—helps me get ready for league night. Wish I coulda had that 300 for league night, though. Maybe now we'll play a little ball—I can't have it getting around the home that I play worse than a girl."

"I don't play ball like a girl and you know it!" Alyssa liked when Pop teased her. He didn't seem so much like an old man then. She felt glad that her Dad had been visiting on Tuesdays; it made her feel better about not brining any extra visitors on Sundays. Maybe next week she would bring Beth. It wasn't like Brent was her only friend.

A few days after the holiday she and Beth saw a movie. "I'm sorry about the whole Spencer thing." She was apologizing as they waited for the popcorn.

"It's cool. I loved the concert. He seemed like a nice enough guy, I'm just not into dating right now."

"I should have known you weren't over Brent yet."

"Technically, I was never under him." Alyssa realized how that sounded. "Oh! You know what I mean."

"So—you haven't talked to Brent yet."

"Nope. Come on, I don't want to miss the trailers." Alyssa tried to walk away, but Beth's legs were more than long enough to keep up.

"You should call him. It could only help things."

"*Things* don't need any help. We are just taking a little break from each other. It's not the big deal you are making it."

"Really? So you haven't been Zombie Alyssa for the past two months?"

"No! I have been concentrating on classes, and I've been busy with family stuff. I really do like the trailers! Let's go."

Okay so the movie wasn't her best idea ever. Beth was great, but too perceptive. Had she really been Zombie Alyssa?

Standing on the porch when Alyssa and Beth got back from the movie theater, were both her parents. Just standing there, in the cold, with no heavy jackets—as if they'd rushed out the door as soon as Beth's car drove into sight. Alyssa and Beth approached the house slowly.

"Something's wrong." Alyssa stated when she and Beth made their way to the front door. "Mom, you're supposed to be at the hospital for another two hours."

"It's your grandfather." Her dad's face looked pained when he spoke.

"Is he in the hospital again?" Alyssa forgot Beth was there and she rushed toward the house.

"Let me grab some things and we'll go see him. I still have his *greatest game* DVDs. Last time they kept him so long and…"

"Alyssa sweetheart." Her mom grabbed her arm before she could get through the door. "He isn't in the hospital. He had a heart attack. There was nothing they could do."

Realization didn't dawn on her until much later that night. She was lying in bed trying to sleep when her thoughts finally made sense again. Her grandfather was gone. She wasn't going to beat him at baseball on Sunday, because she wasn't going to be seeing him on Sunday. She wasn't going to be seeing him at all anymore. The very idea was so foreign that she couldn't process it. All night she'd thought of anything else. She'd made lasagna for dinner. Pop loved her lasagna. No one had eaten much that night. She'd cleaned the bath room. She'd dusted the upstairs banister that her mom always forgot about.

At some point she was pretty sure she'd texted Beth to be sure she got home all right. Alyssa wasn't sure when she'd left. Beth called back, but Alyssa didn't answer. What would she say? So she went to bed. Not to sleep, because she couldn't sleep. She just laid there all night—not sleeping, not thinking, not doing much of anything.

The viewing was more of the same. Alyssa hung up coats, and fetched trays of refreshments. There was a couch reserved for her family. Presumably so other mourners could find them easily and tell them lots of stupid things that wouldn't help at all. So she didn't sit on the couch. Cousins Alyssa couldn't name made conversation with her that she'd never be able to recall. The cousins were all wearing black. Pop hated black on young people. Said it wasn't appropriate for anyone under thirty—Alyssa wasn't sure why that was. She wore her blue skirt.

She didn't think much about Pop. She didn't linger at the photos depicting his life story by the entranceway. She didn't join in while his bowling league from Stoneybrook were swapping stories. She didn't even talk to her dad when he tried to get her to sit down. He was crying. For two days she'd watched him cry for the father he hadn't gotten along with. Alyssa hadn't cried. Not one tear—her mascara was in zero danger. Maybe, she thought briefly, maybe she hadn't loved Pop enough. Or else wouldn't she be crying? When people felt sad they cried. Alyssa couldn't seem to feel sad. She felt frantic and numb and for some reason really-really annoyed—but not sad. Alyssa wished she could sit. Her body was suddenly too heavy—like her legs couldn't support her own weight. No way was she going near that couch.

That night she found herself in bed and wide awake. Again. Maybe she wouldn't ever be able to sleep again. Wasn't there a sixty minutes episode about guy who never slept? She was pretty sure that guy had gone insane. Maybe she would go insane too. Insane people couldn't be expected to go to funerals, could they? Alyssa figured she'd rather go insane than go to the funeral in the morning.

Sometime later, when the pitch black of night had long ago swallowed her room and Alyssa was counting her third flock of sheep, she heard the door creak open. Her mother was being uncharacteristically motherish today. This must be the fifth time she'd been *checked on*.

"Go to bed mom. I'm asleep." She grumbled without turning to face her. There was no answer.

Just when she'd decided her mother must have left, she felt the bed dip behind her. A big heavy arm pulled her against a strong muscular chest and a scratchy cheek rested against her forehead. "I never knew you talked in your sleep." His familiar voice sounded in the dark.

"Brent?"

"Of course Brent. How many men climb into your bed at this hour?" His teasing tone erased weeks of avoiding each other.

"Usually none. I thought we were taking a break?" His warmth felt so good. Suddenly sleep seemed less impossible.

"We're taking a time-out from taking a break." Brent whispered into her hair.

"I'm glad." Alyssa breathed in deeply. "My Pop died." She was much too tired for words like *passed away*.

"I know. Beth called me."

"She has a big mouth."

"Yeah. Lucky isn't it?"

Alyssa couldn't answer. Tears she'd been begging herself to cry for two days suddenly spilled easily down her cheeks. Brent never flinched as she sobbed into his shoulder. He only tucked her blankets in around them, held her tighter, combed his fingers through her hair and murmured reassuring words that made her feel more and more calm. Eventually calm became exhausted and exhausted became asleep.

In the morning she awoke alone in her bed. For a moment she was afraid that it had all been a dream. But before that fear could overtake her she found a post-it note on her mirror.

Went home to shower and change. I'm coming back. We can drive over together.

Alyssa took a deep breath and headed for her own shower. That quiet, calm mood must have been somehow attached to Brent's presence. Now that he was gone the frantic numbness of the day before was settling back in.

She owned two pairs of black dress pants, but just the one navy blue skirt. Probably black slacks were okay as long as she didn't wear a black top too. Didn't she have a dark wine colored sweater somewhere? That sounded somber and appropriate.

"Are just about ready? Your parents just left and…" Brent swung open her bedroom door and immediately turned around to face the hallway. "Sorry, Lyssa." He choked out.

Looking down, Alyssa realized she was standing around in pants and a bra. Where was that sweater? "I don't think I can go. I don't have anything to wear. Pop hates black. I never wear black when I visit. Well I do on game days—Flyers jerseys are the only exception he'll make. So I guess I can't go."

"Lyssa. It doesn't matter what you wear." Brent was still facing the hallway.

"You're probably right. I can wear anything I want—since I am staying home." Brent turned around. He looked incredible. Of course he was wearing black. He only had one suit and it was black. His tie was emerald green. Was it absurd that today of all days she noticed how incredible his eyes looked when he wore that particular shade of green?

"Just stay here a minute, kay?" Brent crossed the room to her window and crawled outside. He must be crazy, Alyssa thought, to be crawling across roof tops in his suit. And she thought she was going insane! A minute later he was climbing back through; only now he was wearing his Flyers Jersey. Wordlessly he crossed to her closet and tossed her jersey over to her. "Get dressed. We are leaving in two minutes."

For some reason this made her feel better. So silently Alyssa scrambled into the jersey, swiped on her lip gloss, and clipped a section of her hair away from her face with a barrette.

"Ready." She turned to face Brent. He was looking at her a little strangely.

"You look beautiful, Lyssa." And he pressed a quick kiss to her forehead.

"You were right. It's a little weird." She mumbled as they walked down the stairs. Behind her he was laughing out loud.

Alyssa wondered if people were staring. By the time they reached the funeral home she'd figured out that people don't normally wear hockey jerseys to funerals. It was strange though, because even while she wondered if they were staring—she didn't really care. When Brent led Alyssa into their seats her father's eyes tried to jump out of his skull. Nope, she still didn't care. Pop would have liked this she thought. Anyway it was the *Pop approved* black, so she was satisfied. Brent wrapped one arm around her shoulder and his free hand squeezed hers throughout the entire service. During the luncheon that followed he never left her side. It was as if he knew she couldn't feel that much needed calmness without him nearby.

In the same way that Alyssa would never recall most of what had been going on over the previous 48 hours, she knew most of this day would also be lost to her. However parts of it would stick with her. And as surely as she knew her own name she knew that 90 years into the future she would be able to recall the exact feeling of Brent's hand holding hers and how his strength seemed to be all that was holding her upright throughout the entire day.

When her obligatory family duties had been fulfilled Brent silently got up from their table and retrieved their coats. She didn't protest that she wanted to stay longer as she probably should have done. Instead she kissed her dad's cheek and told him she'd see him at home.

In the car Alyssa finally found some semblance of a normal voice. "Where did your dad take you this year?" Just because she had recovered the power of intelligent speech didn't mean she was ready to discuss Pop.

"We went north."

"Vague much? Did he take you to meet Santa Claus?"

Brent huffed out a laugh. "Not this trip. We went to Montreal. I could spend a lifetime wandering the old city with my camera."

"Canada? Your dad took you to Canada. Oh my god, and you flew back just for this!"

"Actually I drove. Do you have any idea what a last minute flight from Montreal costs? So I rented a car."

"You drove? Isn't that like a 12 hour drive?"

"Nah, it took about nine. I wanted to be here yesterday—I'm sorry Lyssa."

"You drove nine hours, and you're sorry you were late? Well gee, I guess I'll let you slide this time." Brent chuckled a little. "I'm a little surprised my parents let you in last night. What time was it?"

"It was late and I didn't exactly ask permission." Alyssa raised her eyebrows at him. "Your dad answered the door, and let me upstairs. He could have asked me to leave if he wanted to. Not that I would have." The last part he seemed to be whispering to himself.

Alyssa took a few moments to digest that information. There didn't seem to be much left to say, so she moved on. "About before…"

"It's a time-out Lyssa. We don't have to do this now. We'll get around to it, but this isn't the time."

"Thanks." She shouldn't have let that be the end of it. But she was a coward, and she wasn't ready to call an end to their time-out. "So tell me about Canada."

"I'll do better than that...I brought my camera back with me." Back at Alyssa's house they plugged his camera into her big screen TV. And Alyssa lost herself in the beauty of Old Montreal, Mount Royal, and The Montmorency Falls. For hours they clicked through thousands of photos and she enjoyed his company refusing to acknowledge the new level of intimacy presumed when he tucked her body against his on the couch— her back to his chest with his arms circled tightly around her waist. If she thought too hard about how closely he was holding her or about how she'd spent an entire night using his chest instead of her pillow she would probably have to pull away and restore an appropriate distance. At the moment, she needed his closeness more than she needed her next breath.

Eventually the evening came to an end. "I'm driving back tomorrow. I promised my Dad I'd be back for New Years."

"You are always home for New Years."

"This year I came home early. So Dad gets a couple extra days in exchange."

Alyssa nodded. That made perfect sense. She was out of time. "So you're leaving?"

A smile twitched around at the edges of his mouth. "I don't think your dad would be cool about any more sleepovers. I'm not sure my just-try-and-stop-me act would fly tonight."

"Oh. Of course. Good night." Alyssa collapsed on the inside. She was going to have to face another night. What had she expected?

Brent tilted his head thoughtfully "'night Lyssa" and he left.

When Alyssa turned off her light that night she rolled over in bed preparing to face the endless hours ahead of her. Someone knocked on the door. No, it was the window. She wasted no time in letting Brent in.

"Did you forget something?"

Brent shook his head. "You should have seen your face downstairs. I felt like I was kicking a puppy." He slipped off his shoes and shrugged out of his coat before pulling her down onto the bed with him.

His big body curled around hers and she breathed a contented sigh. Tomorrow she would face the world. Not tonight. "Thanks."

"Just go to sleep Chere." He kissed her temple, and she closed her eyes.

His weight against her body and the tight arm around her waist were just as comforting as they'd been the night before. Only now at the edges of that comfort was a little something else. And it was a bit difficult to fall asleep. Not the same difficult as if she'd been alone, but an exciting kind of difficult that she worked really hard to ignore. Because Brent had the right of it earlier that day in his car—now was not the time.

"Lyssa. Wake up." Brent's hoarse whisper and a gentle shaking broke her into awareness. The early morning sun was still orange where it streamed into her bedroom. Brent was crouched next to the bed, his coat already on.

"What time is it?"

"Not quite six. I'm leaving."

"So early? Come on—I'll make you breakfast." Alyssa started to swing her legs onto the floor.

"No. I'm gonna go out the window. I don't want your dad to know I was here."

"He knew the last time."

Brent leveled a look at her that meant she was missing something he considered to be rather obvious. "He knew before I came upstairs. And I used the front door."

"Nothing happened."

He considered her for a moment like he was weighing his next words. "It isn't *respectful* Lyssa—to crawl through a girl's window and spend the night with her."

"Nothing happened!"

Brent clamped a hand over her mouth. "I gotta go. You can call me anytime." He released her now that she wasn't shouting. "You should have been the one to call before, not Beth. You know that right?"

"I wasn't sure." Alyssa chewed on her lip. They weren't supposed to do this yet. It wasn't the right time—his words!

"Always. You can always call me." He hugged her. "We still need to talk; you know that too, right?" She nodded against his shoulder. "Okay. Good enough. I'll be back in a couple of days."

Then he was gone.

Chapter Fourteen

New Years was over and the last of the Christmas decorations were away. Brent of course was home. His classes would have resumed by now— Alyssa's had. But he didn't call. Alyssa figured their *break* was back on. Beth had been very apologetic about overstepping her bounds and calling Brent. Alyssa didn't mention that she was sure she wouldn't have made it through the funeral without him. Actually she didn't mention that he'd come home at all. This wasn't because she wanted Beth to feel guilty. It was simply because all things *Brent* made her head ache these days. If he wanted to have that talk with her he could call, because she couldn't handle it.

A few weeks into the school year Alyssa allowed Beth to drag her to a party. "It's the last weekend before we start cheering again. We'll go to the party—and then you can spend the night with me." She'd pleaded. Alyssa agreed to meet them there. Mostly because she figured she could change her mind later. So it was sort of a letdown when Tommy's car pulled into the drive that evening. Apparently Beth didn't think she could be trusted to show up—perceptive, remember?

The party should have been fun. She used to love going to these things. A few months ago she would have seen a room full of her closest friends, but now she just saw a bunch of people trying too hard. Beth and Tommy were somewhere dancing. Alyssa wandered into another room looking for drinks. There were usually a few coolers of soft drinks somewhere.

"Beer, Lyssa?" Stupidly hopeful Alyssa spun around. It was Pete. He was standing in the doorway smiling and holding out a can of beer to her. As if it was still September, and he still had a reason to be talking to her.

"That isn't a nickname I tolerate from just anybody." She said coldly.

Pete ignored her demeanor. "Let's be friends again. Wanna dance?"

"I don't think so." Alyssa moved to walk past him. Pete sidestepped to block her way.

"Jenn says Carter dropped you, huh? That's okay. I think you and I should give it another go. Prom is only a few months away you know."

It was four months away—that was twice as long as their relationship had lasted in the first place. "Don't believe everything Jenn has to say." Alyssa tried to push past again.

Pete blocked her and shoved the beer into her hands. "She's not here tonight—probably on another date with Carter. She just can't stop talking about her *Hillfield man*."

Suddenly Alyssa was angry with Brent. This was his fault. In September she would have been perfectly happy to spend the evening sipping a beer and dancing with the most popular boy is school. Now he'd ruined that for her, and was possibly out with Jennifer Pastings. Alyssa took the beer.

Two beers later she and Pete left the dance floor and found a private room to talk in. It looked like someone's home office. "How was your holiday?" He was asking her even as he trapped her against a wall and leaned in for a kiss.

"This is a bad idea." Alyssa ducked under one of his arms and put several feet of distance between them. "I'm drunk."

"So am I." Pete advanced toward her. "Don't tell me you weren't hooking up with Carter. I've seen you crawling through his window."

"That's none of your business! When did you see me?" The room was spinning a little. Alyssa really hated beer.

"I drive by your house sometimes." Pete's smile took on a creepy slant. He was a more practiced drunk than Alyssa—so when he lurched towards her she wasn't able to avoid his grasp.

Taking down a small end table as they fell, Alyssa and Pete tumbled to the carpet together—her arm twisting awkwardly between their bodies. She considered panicking. He was everywhere and a lot stronger than her too. Man did she hate that about him! She decided against panicking. Her knee came up hard between his legs and she scrambled towards the door.

"Shit! Alyssa!" Pete howled and curled into a fetal position. Tommy must have been passing by because he had the door open before Alyssa's hand closed around the knob.

"Beth's looking for you." He said pushing Alyssa out of the doorway behind him. Tommy took a few steps into the room and righted the fallen table. On his way back out the door, the toe of his heavy boot caught Pete's rib cage. "Oops." He muttered darkly as he joined Alyssa and Beth in the hall.

"What happened?" Beth was screeching.

"I don't know. Pete tried to kiss me I guess." Alyssa mumbled to her friend. She was trying to decide if she wanted to get sick. No, she didn't think so.

"We're leaving." Tommy took both girls' arms and steered them out the front door.

In the car Alyssa was left alone in the back seat with her thoughts. Damn, Brent! If she'd known their friendship was ruined anyway, she would have kissed him in the car that night. What a waste. This was clearly his fault. If they hadn't been so close in the first place she wouldn't have needed a fake boyfriend and she wouldn't have minded Pete kissing her tonight. Now she didn't have a boyfriend or a best friend. Nope, no kissing for Alyssa.

In between her irrational musings some of the conversation from the front seat filtered back to her.

"She's supposed to go to my house."

"Your mom'll never let her past the front door. How much did she drink? I don't think I've ever seen her finish even one beer."

"I didn't see how many she had. She doesn't drink. We can't take her home—her parents will kill her!"

Geez! Was everyone extra notice-y lately, or was she that bad of an actor? Why did she even bother? She could have avoided that whole embarrassing scene months ago when Brent poured out her drink in the grass. Alyssa fumed a little in the back seat.

"Is there a back door? Maybe we could sneak her in?"

"I can hear you, you know." Alyssa interrupted them. Tommy's eyes focused on her in the rearview mirror for a moment; he actually did seem surprised that she could hear them. "Just take me home. I'll be fine."

When they turned onto her street Alyssa noticed Brent's house was dark. His car was in the drive, but his mother's wasn't. Maybe Jenn had picked him up? It was too early for him to be home from a date already. "Let me out here."

Tommy pulled over in front of Brent's house. "It looks dark." He sounded skeptical about letting her out.

"There's a hide-a-key under the porch swing."

Tommy nodded resignedly and waited until she was inside the Carter's front door before pulling away.

Alyssa didn't bother with any lights. She knew this house as well as her own. She would just nap in Brent's bed until he came back from his date, and by then she'd be sober enough to go home. It was a good plan.

"What the! Alyssa?" Brent bolted upright when she crawled onto the bed.

"You're not supposed to be here." Alyssa mumbled at him. He wasn't wearing a shirt. He'd been fully clothed both times he'd shared her bed last month. Actually he'd been sleeping in his jeans and tee shirt those nights. That was probably unusual. Boy he smelled good.

"Where else would I be? Are you okay?"

"Yup." Alyssa considered him for a moment. "I wish I'd kissed you after the dance." Alyssa leaned forward and kissed him.

He still tasted like toothpaste; probably he hadn't been in bed long. His large muscled arms reached out and tugged her the rest of the way into his bed. She remembered this. The warmth of his skin penetrating through her clothes and the feel of his weight pressing her into the mattress were both familiar and new at the same time. She felt dizzy. Well she'd been feeling a little dizzy since Pete had brought her that second drink, but this was a better dizzy. Brent rolled her body more completely under his. Alyssa cried out.

"What?" Brent levered himself off of her. "Are you all right...Jesus! What's wrong with your arm?"

Alyssa looked down to where his eyes were fixed on her arm between their bodies. It did look kind of swollen and red...oh right. "Someone fell on it." She reached up to kiss him again.

Chapter Fifteen

The sun was brighter than usual, and someone was pounding on the door. No. The pounding was in her head and there was an awful taste in her mouth. Why couldn't she move? Alyssa shook herself more fully awake. Brent's thick arm was pinned around her waist where she was wearing a large green tee shirt. Crap. This was Brent's room. Shifting slightly she felt a damp spot on the sheets against her side. Wide eyed, Alyssa's eyes shot downward. Oh. There was a melted icepack strapped to her arm. The bendy kind with Velcro straps. Last night's activities rushed back to her.

The party. Pete being a jackass. Getting into bed with Brent. Alyssa eased Brent's arm to one side and slipped out of bed. Cold morning air tingled on her bare legs. What had she done? Stupid question, she chided herself as she spied her jeans in a pile at the foot of the bed. She knew exactly what she'd done. But what had she been thinking! Any hope she'd had for saving their friendship was out the window now. The window! Alyssa hopped into her pants and crawled out his window.

Back in her own room she exchanged his green lantern tee shirt for her flannel pajama top and crawled into her own bed. Immediately she got back out of bed and flipped the lock on her window—just in case. Back in bed she pulled the covers tightly over her head and willed herself to fall back asleep. What was she going to do now? Everything was so screwed up. She hated Pete for bringing her that beer. Why had she taken it anyway? Right, he'd brought up Jenn.

"Oh man." Alyssa moaned out loud when she realized that Brent had been out on a date with Jenn just before she'd accosted him in his bed.

Her stomach turned over. She wasn't sure if it was the hang over or if it was more about Jennifer Pastings. Alyssa forced several deep breaths into her lungs. She remembered thinking his breath tasted minty, and felt and absurd rush of relief that he'd at least brushed his teeth between girls. Her life was ruined. She'd never be able to cheer on the same squad as Jennifer this semester. Although having a quasi-reasonable reason to quit the squad was a bit of a relief. That would definitely be the last party she'd go to with Beth and Tommy. So there went her social life.

Not that it was either Beth or Tommy's fault—she'd behaved like an idiot. But still she could hardly expect Beth to start skipping parties, and doing what? Ordering pizzas with her? Nope. Her social life had definitely come to a crashing halt. It was only four months until graduation. She didn't really need a social life. Feeling strangely relieved that her future as a social reject was decided Alyssa finally drifted off into sleep.

She stayed in bed all day. Not that Sundays were all that busy for her these days anyway. She woke up long enough to silence her phone when Brent called and again in the afternoon when her mother shook her awake and asked about the night before. She seemed pretty well satisfied with Alyssa's story that the grocery store sushi bar had messed with her stomach and that she'd asked Beth to bring her home late in the night. If her mother were more observant she might wonder why there was a man's green lantern tee shirt lying in the middle of her daughter's floor, but thank goodness for small favors.

In the afternoon her mom knocked on the door again. Brent was at the front door, and did Alyssa feel well enough for visitors? Nope. She was much too sick for company.

"Honey, did you forget to set your alarm? You'll be late." Alyssa opened her eyes to see her mother standing in the bedroom doorway.

It must be morning again. Monday. School. Lame. "I'm too sick for school today mom."

Her mother gave her a disbelieving look, but there was sympathy in it too. "Is there something you want to talk about sweetheart?"

"I'm just sick mom. I have a temperature."

"*Really?*" Parents shouldn't use sarcasm. It is a young person's tool.

"Yes. *Really*. It's one thousand and four. I'd probably faint in the middle of English class." Alyssa pulled her blanket up higher and rolled towards the wall.

"Okay, I'll call the school"

Alyssa waited until she heard two cars pull out the drive before wandering down to the kitchen and polishing off three half full take out containers of Chinese food. She was still wearing her blue jeans from Saturday night. Sleeping in blue jeans was not something she would recommend. Upstairs, Alyssa striped down for a shower. For the first time she actually looked at her arm with sober eyes. A disgusting splotchy purple bruise was spread over her entire forearm. No wonder it had been feeling tender. Flexing and rolling it experimentally Alyssa satisfied herself that it wasn't broken or seriously injured.

At least the weather was still cold. She could hide her arm under long sleeves until it cleared up. After her shower she slathered a chamomile and vitamin k cream on her arm, pulled on a fresh long sleeved shirt, and climbed back into bed.

On Tuesday morning her fever was gone, but she felt quite sure her tonsils were swelling up. Surprisingly her mother agreed that it would be irresponsible for her to spread potential germs around school. In the afternoon Beth brought her homework by the house. Alyssa made her leave it on the dresser by the doorway. To save her from the dreaded germs, of course.

"I'm not going to ask you what happened. You can tell me when you're ready. But you should answer your phone. I called all morning. You're inbox is full."

Alyssa flopped her arm over the side of the bed, and groped around on the floor until her fingers brushed against the phone—still where she'd left in Sunday morning. It was dead. "I wasn't ignoring you, it just died and I didn't realize that's all." Beth rolled her eyes and left.

Alyssa plugged in her phone. She had over 30 missed calls. Her voicemail box was indeed full. She pressed play.

"Lyssa, call me back."

"Lyssa. It's Brent. Are you okay?"

"Why wouldn't you see me? I'm sorry about last night. Please call me back."

"Stop being weird and call me back."

"Beth says you weren't in school. Is your arm okay? I should have looked at it better."

"Please, Lyssa!"

"Okay, remember when you were worried about things being weird. We passed weird about 18 hours ago."

"I can't believe you locked the window! I didn't even know that damn lock worked"

"Whatever. You are being childish and melodramatic. I don't find it cute anymore' Lyssa."

"_____" His last message was just empty air. Alyssa could almost hear him sighing and rolling his eyes.

Maybe it seemed childish to him, but this was old territory for him! Not that she'd been saving herself exactly. But it would be nice to actually be able to remember what it had been like. She didn't even know if she liked it or not. Although judging by the butterflies she hadn't been able to shake since November she was pretty sure she had liked it. Probably, she liked it a lot.

On Wednesday her Dad came in instead of her mother. "Hey buttercup." She hated that nickname. "How're you feeling today?"

"Bronchitis?" She tried weakly.

He shook his head. "If you like I can stay home from work today. We can go see a doctor."

"I don't think I need antibiotics or anything."

"I don't think so either. That isn't exactly the kind of doctor I was thinking of."

Oh-my-god! He wanted to take her to a shrink. Not that there was anything wrong with that. Actually she knew a couple of kids who had seen therapists. Mostly post divorce stuff when they were in grade school, but still. "I'm fine Dad."

"I understand if you don't want to talk about it with me."

Eww. Of course she wasn't going to talk about it with her dad!

"But I know how you felt about him." He was still talking. How did he know? Even Alyssa didn't know how she felt about Brent. "We weren't always very close, but he was my dad you know? I miss him very much." Pop. Her dad thought she'd spent three days in bed because of Pop.

Guilt stampeded through Alyssa's heart. She hadn't thought of him once since Saturday night. She was too wrapped up in her own drama. Damn. Brent was right, she was acting childishly.

"I know you do Dad. I'm sorry if I've been acting umm...childishly." This seemed to catch him off guard. "I'm going to school. I feel much better this morning."

When her dad left, Alyssa headed for a shower. Her arm was a patchwork of greens and browns today. That vitamin K cream was such a crock. After a much needed rinse and repeat (it was gross how grimy you could get just from laying in bed) and after choosing a simple blue long sleeve shirt to go with her jeans and sneakers, Alyssa went to school.

At her locker before homeroom Alyssa felt many eyes on her. But it was possible that was just her inner drama queen. They couldn't know any better than her dad could have known.

"Hey Alyssa." She turned to find Pete shifting awkwardly from one foot to another next to her. His face was black and blue on one side and he had a thin splint taped to his nose.

"Hey Pete."

"Umm...about your arm—it was an accident. I mean...I wouldn't have hurt you."

Alyssa didn't have any emotions to spare for being angry with Pete and they'd both been drunk. "The arm's fine. Better than your nose anyway. What happened there?"

Pete's eyes narrowed a little. "You didn't hear?"

"Nope, I've been sick."

"I got sacked. On Sunday, in a game at the park."

"Sucks." Alyssa turned back to her locker.

"So, friends again?" Pete was smiling at her. Had she ever really found that smile appealing?

"Nope." Alyssa closed her locker door. "We never really were Pete. And just so we're clear—driving by my house is not okay. Actually it's a little stalker-y"

"Right. You got it." Pete raised his hands, backed off and walked away. That went easier than she'd originally expected it too.

After school she stayed late to hunt down Miss Barb the Cheer coach. Quitting the squad was a little more difficult than blowing off Pete. Apparently being chosen as head cheerleader was a big honor and she had a responsibility to her friends. Alyssa was suddenly struck by the thought that the only friend she had on the squad was Beth. "You should think about appointing Beth. She'd do a much better job than I ever did." There, responsibility fulfilled.

With that taken care of Alyssa felt relieved and terrified at the same time. She wouldn't have any reason to deal with Jenn any time soon, but she also was looking at a lot of empty afternoons. At least she would have time for homework. Maybe Brent was right, and her grades would improve with better study habits. Oops, she hadn't meant to think about the B word.

After a couple of weeks she realized that there was probably a little something to Brent's studying theory. Now that she had zero social life her grades were picking up. She'd had a pop quiz in English class on the *Canterville Ghost* and she didn't even break a sweat. It was really too bad that colleges didn't pay much attention to the end of your senior year. She bet she could get herself accepted to Penn State based just on that quiz. It was almost definitely going to be an A. Brent would have been proud of her. If they were speaking—which they weren't. He'd stopped calling. Alyssa wouldn't know what to say if she called him, so she didn't.

At the end of chemistry class one day Beth jogged to catch up to Alyssa in the hallway. "Are you still angry with me for dragging you to that party? Cause I think Pete got what he deserved." Alyssa smiled a little remembering Tommy's swift kick to his ribs.

"I was never mad. You didn't force me to drink, or to dance with my ex-boyfriend."

"So why aren't you talking to me then?"

"What are you talking about?"

"Duh! You haven't said two words to me since that day I brought your homework after school. At first I thought it must have something to do with Brent. He seemed concerned you weren't calling him back…"

"When did you talk to Brent?" Alyssa wasn't very sure she liked the idea of Brent talking about her to anyone else.

"He's just worried about you. Cut him some slack. But what about me? I miss you."

"I miss you too. But I don't really miss cheering. I am thinking of taking up a new hobby."

Beth looked confused. "What does that have to do with anything?"

"Well you're busy being the new head cheerleader—congrats by the way—and I am going to be busy with, whatever. I haven't thought of a new hobby yet."

"So you don't want to hang out because we are going to be doing different extra curriculars? Didn't you ever have friends that weren't on the squad?"

"No. Well—Brent."

Beth was shaking her head. "Okay. This afternoon, you, me, and my new spring wardrobe. Meet me at the mall?"

"I'd like that yeah." Wow. Maybe she could still have a social life.

Alyssa thought about that on her drive home after school. Why *had* she thought Beth wouldn't have time for her if she wasn't wearing a cheer skirt anymore? Beth wasn't that shallow. Uh-oh. Maybe she was the one that was shallow. It did seem a little over the top now—that she'd made Brent trail after her at social events like an accessory to her cheerleading uniform.

She was single now, and it was hardly powering any major rumor mill. Of course she was no longer a part of Jenn's inner circle so there was the distinct possibility that the rumors were out there. But if she didn't have to listen to them did she really care?

Man! Brent was just getting righter and righter. At least one benefit to not speaking to him was that she did not have to hear him say I-told-you-so. Of course Brent wasn't really the I-told-you-so kind of person. Okay so new plan: instead of lying around waiting for graduation Alyssa would—what? Well something not shallow that's for sure.

Chapter Sixteen

"Didn't you need anything?" Beth's voice was coming through a dressing room door. Alyssa stood in the small waiting area guarding Beth's already significant pile of bags.

"Not as much as you." She joked.

"I like clothes." Beth wasn't offended in the least. "Anyway—my dad pays my credit card and he can afford it."

Alyssa giggled a little. Her parents could afford it too, but that didn't mean she was going to rush out and run up a credit card bill. Of course her parents would never give her a credit card to begin with, so the point was moot.

They were having a great time. There wasn't a store in the mall they'd left out. Even Pam's pet emporium had warranted a visit. The kittens were so cute! Alyssa had missed fun. It was possible, she realized, that she'd been wallowing a little bit in her own drama.

"So tell me about this new hobby." Beth asked when they'd settled themselves in front burgers and fries in the food court.

"Nothing to tell at the moment. I just have a lot of free time on my hands at the moment. Maybe I'll get a part time job or go out for softball." Even as she said it Alyssa was deciding against working. The money would be nice, but somehow that didn't seem to fulfill her non-shallow requirements.

"Umm…Alyssa? Softball tryouts were last week. I don't think any of the sports teams are open."

Oh. Well sports weren't really nonshallow either. Too bad though. Softball sounded like fun. "Okay—I'll think of something." Alyssa put on a bright smile, but this was hard.

It took a few weeks of empty afternoons, but Alyssa finally thought of something. She suddenly remembered that Brent had been very impressed when she worked at the hospital's carnival. It was fun too. Probably growing as a person wasn't supposed to be and fun, but if it was good enough to impress Brent…Brent was definitely the least shallow person she knew. Or used to know, since they weren't really friends anymore.

You have to take a class to be a candy striper. That's what the hospital volunteers are called. The woman who answered when Alyssa called the hospital about volunteering explained that to her. Taking the class wouldn't be such a big deal since it was on Saturdays and Alyssa's weekends tended to be wide open lately, but the next class wasn't until May. So Alyssa signed up, but she was still facing eight weeks of boring until then. Beth thought it was great though. Cheerleading would be over by then, so Beth was free to sign up too.

The next day Alyssa decided to try the library. Volunteering at the library wouldn't be as interesting, but it would be *volunteering* and so it would fit her agenda just as well.

The library had a waiting list of people wanting to do volunteer work. A waiting list! That many people wanted to spend their weekends alphabetizing books—or dewey decimalizing books? Whatever. She was worthless. No one needed her help. Alyssa briefly considered crawling back into her bed for another three days. That would probably be back sliding, so instead she went to the park. She would go for a run—she needed to try and stay in shape somehow now that she was a couch potato.

Next to the parking lot at the local park was a paved quarter mile track that circled a big playground—no one was interested in monkey bars today. It wasn't that warm. A little further from the parked cars were a couple of sports fields. As a kid she'd come here to play soccer, softball, and any other sport her parents would sign her up for. Brent was terrible at soccer but he'd made his mom bring him to all the games anyway.

Running was boring. Alyssa loved pretty much every sport—except the ones you did alone. This sucks, she thought as she took her third lap around the track. Not even a whole mile, and she was bored. Probably she'd only made it this far because the park was very pretty and she'd been admiring the view. Spring wasn't here yet, but it was a warm march and the grass was looking green again.

Alyssa strained her eyes to see a couple of people on the baseball diamond. As the straightaway of the track brought her closer she made out a small figure wildly swinging a bat in front of the backstop. It couldn't be entirely his fault that he hadn't hit a single ball because the pitcher looked even more awkward than the kid. When the track curved Alyssa veered off into the grass and headed towards the ball field.

Closer up, she could tell that the child was actually a she. A little girl of about nine years with a blond ponytail pulled messily through the back of red Phillies cap was staring determinedly at the pitcher. Alyssa assumed the older woman was the girl's mother. The mother was only standing about 20 feet from home plate—nowhere near the pitcher's mound. She still couldn't seem to get the ball into the strike zone. Alyssa watched for a little while longer. The backstop behind, and in front of, the girl became littered with softballs. She hadn't hit even one.

"Hi there." Alyssa smiled brightly and waved to the pitcher as she approached the girl. "I'm Alyssa." Now she was speaking to the mom.

The older woman jogged over. "Nice to meet you, I'm Patty, and this is my daughter Lynn." The little girl looked up at her shyly from beneath her cap.

"Hey there, Lynn." Alyssa crouched down to look her in the eye. "Do you like softball? I do."

"I don't know. We haven't started yet."

"She's signed up for the rec league, they start next week. We were just practicing a bit." Patty put in.

"I played for the rec league when I was your size. It's fun."

"Is it?" The girl's eyes went as wide as saucers. "It isn't hard?"

"Well it wouldn't be very fun if it was too easy. If your mommy doesn't mind. Maybe I could show you a couple of tricks."

Patty's face colored with relief and appreciation.

"Alright. Well I'll let you in on a secret. The most important thing to remember when you're hitting? Your elbow." Alyssa adjusted the girls batting stance and helped her choke up on the bat.

After a few swings Alyssa tactfully gave Patty a break from pitching. Lynn was doing much better now that she knew where to hold the bat and of course now that she had something worth hitting. She still had trouble, but each time her bat made that thud of contact with the ball her smile more than made up for any strikes. It wasn't just her smiling either. Alyssa was as happy for her as Patty. Before she knew it dusk was chasing them back to their cars.

"Can you come next week too? That's the real practice." Lynn wanted to know.

"Umm. I'm not sure your coach would appreciate that. But good luck, I know you are going to love playing softball."

"Actually." Patty cleared her throat. "We completely appreciated your help today and you probably are very busy, but the assistant coach just backed out. I was going to volunteer but I realize now that I'm in over my head. If you're interested…"

"Yes!" Alyssa was embarrassed at how loud she'd been. "I mean, yes I am interested. I've been…umm…looking for a volunteer opportunity so, yes. I am interested."

Patty beamed at her. "You must be looking to pad those college applications huh? Well we would love to have you." She fished a business card out of her purse. "Here's my contact information. Give me a call and I will put you in contact with Sherry Palm—our coach."

Alyssa could have danced home. As a matter of fact she did do quite a bit of bopping around to the radio in the car. When she pulled into her driveway she was in such a good mood she almost didn't bother to check Brent's driveway for his car or Jenn's car. *Almost.*

Chapter Seventeen

Normally she wasn't a big fan of bright red. But Alyssa was very pleased with her new *Ladybugs* team shirt. She would be leaving for the park in just a minute. The Ladybugs had their first game this morning. Coaching was more fun than Alyssa had anticipated. Hanging out with those girls was becoming something she very much looked forward to all week. Alyssa tried not to think of herself as pathetic for enjoying the company of a bunch of fourth graders. They were all just so ready to have a good time. No one was worried about gossip, or boyfriends, or breaks, or time-outs. Alyssa decided she hadn't appreciated the fourth grade nearly enough while she was there.

They didn't just goof off either. Every one of those girls showed up to their twice a week practices ready to work. Lynn was still having a little trouble at bat, but she was by far the team's best catcher. Another little girl named Sammie was quickly developing a promising pitch and Alyssa had high hopes for today's game. Of course at nine years old she was sure the girls would bounce back quickly from a loss, but they totally deserved a win.

Adjusting her hat on her head, Alyssa headed out to her car. She was going to be so early, but she was too excited to wait around anymore. Her spirits came crashing down around her when she saw Brent leaving his front door at the same time she left hers. Taking a step backwards Alyssa intended to escape back inside her front door until he'd gone, but it was too late. Brent's eyes found her and he altered his path to intercept hers.

What did he want? What could she say to him? It had been over two months since they'd…well what was there to say? He looked good. His hair was too long—he tended to forget when it was time for a trip to the barber. At this length his hair was starting to curl. Alyssa loved those curls.

"How are you, Alyssa?"

"Oh. Umm. I'm good. You?" Weird. Weird. Weird!

"I've been better." Brent sighed. He was so not allowed to sigh at her anymore. She was experiencing major personal growth here!

"I quit cheering."

"Yeah. I heard about that." Probably from Jenn.

"I'm coaching a softball team now." Well assistant coaching, but whatever.

"I heard that too." Where did Jenn get her information from? Oh, well. At least he was smiling now. "Lyssa, can we—"

Alyssa cut him off. "I'm sorry, Brent. I've got to run or I'll be late for the game. I'll see you okay?"

Like the coward that she was, Alyssa hightailed it to her car leaving Brent staring after her on the sidewalk. Maybe she should have let him finish his sentence. Maybe he'd been about to say *let's just go back to being best friends.* As much as Alyssa missed her friendship with Brent she knew there were some things they couldn't come back from and drunken sex was at the top of that list. Maybe he's been about to profess his undying love to her. But she wasn't sure she wanted that either. Well okay she was pretty sure she did, but what if it was still weird? Then where would they be?

He'd smiled though. Perhaps he was a little impressed? That idea pleased her and while her excitement from earlier that morning wasn't entirely restored, she did perk up a little. The Ladybugs won. And Alyssa's inner cheerleader burst out when Lynn hit a homerun in the first inning. It probably should have been a double—but nine year olds suck at fielding. Over all it was a banner day in spite of her Brent moment. That moment had clung to her all day. She couldn't help thinking that he would have enjoyed the game.

Brent hit like a girl, but he threw a wicked curveball. Of course this was slow pitch softball for fourth graders and no one threw curveballs, but still. Alyssa spared a few minutes to regret rushing off on him. She was very aware that the last six months had been all her fault. And a painful game of *what if* kept playing mercilessly in her head. What if she'd kissed him in the car that night, if she'd called him when Pop died, if she'd just been straight with people about their relationship in the first place. Then Brent would have been with her today. Cheering for Lynn, and offering to buy her celebratory pizza after the win.

Not that she needed Brent to indulge in celebratory pizza. But even after all this personal growth, she still wasn't planning to be seen at a pizza place stuffing her face—alone. Weren't there some frozen pizza pockets at home? Yes. That's what she would do. Pizza pockets and a good book. Alyssa hadn't made time for much reading since the eighth grade. Now she was on the third twilight book—boy had she been missing out. A Saturday night playing Jacob or Edward over her microwaved dinner? Not lame. Personally she favored Jacob. He was more fun. Alyssa missed fun.

On Sunday Alyssa woke up with a stomach ache. Stupid pizza pockets. Sundays used to be her favorite part of the week. She knew it was unusual that her best friend next to Brent had always been her grandfather, but that never used to bother her. Now she didn't have either of them. Or Mr. Petry, or Mrs. Sloan, Alyssa even missed Charles. Even though at thirty she thought he was too old to flirt with her the way he did, and way too young to be dismissed into the same category of Mr. Petry. The old Alyssa would have brooded at the unfairness in life. New Alyssa decided to swing by Stoneybrook and have a visit.

Walking into the building was more difficult than she'd expected. After the receptionist's initial surprise at seeing her after all this time things got better. She signed Mrs. Sloan's visitor book and went upstairs to find out how her grandson was liking married life.

"Didn't you know dear? They are expecting! Imagine, me a *great-grandmother*." Mrs. Sloan continued on about the baby blanket she was already at work on, and green was a neutral color so it wouldn't matter boy or girl. "It ain't natural this *finding out*. No, I told them I don't want to know. I can be surprised when the time comes just like god intended. There is a reason you know that he didn't put a window in women's stomachs."

Alyssa pretty sure there were other logistical issues with the whole window thing. But it was a sweet sentiment, and she wondered if, one day when she was *expecting*, she would be able to wait for the surprise. Probably not—patience was not among her virtues.

"Where is that young man friend of yours these days?"

"hmm? Oh. Brent and I—well it's just me today." Alyssa finished lamely.

"So it's like that is it? I thought something was funny when he started showing up in the week and you were still coming on Sundays."

"Brent? My friend came to visit you? Tall, blond, green eyes?"

"No need to describe him to me! These are new glasses and my mind's as sharp as a tack."

"I'm sorry ma'am I didn't mean to offend. I just wasn't aware Brent had been to visit you that's all."

"Not me, deary—although bless his soul he always stopped to say hello, and I never turn down a visitor. But no it was Al he was visiting. Started coming on Tuesdays; I could hear that TV game all the way down this end of the hall..."

She kept talking, but Alyssa lost her ability to listen. Brent had been to visit Pop. Often—by the sound of it. She remembered when Pop started confusing him with her father, but she hadn't put it together at Christmas when Pop claimed her dad came on Tuesdays. She should have, since no way would her dad spend an evening playing Wii Bowling. Was it really possible that she'd missed his exact level of wonderfulness all these years? Now that she was aware of it there wasn't a whole lot she could do about it.

Alyssa visited with Mrs. Sloan a little longer and then she walked around and popped in on the few other people she knew. When Mrs. Sloan said what she did about not turning away visitors, it occurred to her that maybe she wasn't the only one in the world to feel lonely. All the residents were very happy to see her, and no one said anything dumb about being *sorry for her loss.* In a way that was sad, because it just meant that these people had grown used to losing loved ones. But mostly it was a relief to be able to talk about Pop without having to talk about his death. Mr. Petry offered to play her in game of chess, but that was something about Sundays she hadn't missed. New Alyssa didn't like losing anymore than old Alyssa had.

Alyssa turned 18 on the warmest sunniest April day she could ever remember. Usually her birthday called for boots and an umbrella. This year she pulled out open toed sandals and a sundress. Now—warm sunny days in April are still *days in April,* so she pulled a light sweater over the spaghettis straps of her dress. Sweater and all she felt very springish and was determined to enjoy the day. After all you only turn 18 once.

Last year on her birthday Alyssa found her car filled to the brim with balloons when she left for school in the morning. This year it was much easier climbing into her car. At sixteen she almost missed homeroom after spending the morning over a tall stack of homemade, strawberry, birthday pancakes. Who needed all those calories?

At school Beth and Tommy were waiting by her locker with chocolate chip muffins.

"Oh wow, thanks guys!" Alyssa took a huge bite. "So much better than pancakes." She grinned at them.

"Happy birthday, you're welcome, and what about pancakes?" Beth smiled widely from where she was leaning against Tommy leaning against the row of lockers.

"Never mind." Alyssa smiled to herself around a second bite.

"So what's on the agenda for the evening?" Tommy wanted to know.

"Well it's a Friday night, and my mom has a late shift at the hospital so that means I'll be fixing my own dinner, doing homework and going to bed early." Alyssa groused. The Ladybugs did have a game the next day, so it wasn't as if her entire weekend was a bust. But it was still a pretty depressing plan for her 18th birthday. Last September she and

Brent had driven all over town buying lottery tickets…just because he could.

"Or, you could come out with us." Beth linked her arm through Alyssa's and started off down the hallway. "And that is more of a demand than a request. I have been planning a surprise for you."

"I'd listen to her, Alyssa. She's getting bossy in her old age." Tommy teased. Beth had celebrated her 18th birthday at the end of January. Tommy, like Brent, was born in September. Alyssa suspected he missed lording his *legal* status over them.

Beth continued on as if he hadn't spoken. "We were going to leave right after school, but you can't wear that."

Alyssa was insulted. "I like this dress!"

"It's a nice dress, but you are going to want pants, and a jacket." They were passing Beth and Tommy's homeroom, so Alyssa didn't get a chance to question the cryptic comment.

A surprise sounded nice. Most of the rest of the day Alyssa enjoyed herself. In other years she had gone out of her way to flaunt her birthday with beauty queen style birthday girl sashes, and carrying around flowers or gifts that she'd hinted shamelessly to various boys about. It was a surprise when she realized she didn't miss the constant comments and good wishes those tactics had brought her. Her closer friends remembered, and it turned out that those were the only *happy birthdays* she needed. She left her phone on all day. The school had very strict rules against this, but Brent might remember it was her birthday, and text her or something. So she left it on. He didn't.

After school Beth and Tommy followed her home, and Beth insisted she change into jeans and sneakers. And a jacket.

"Gee mom, should I wear a hat?" Alyssa teased as they climbed into Tommy's car.

"Nah, helmets are provided." Beth tossed a cryptic look back to where she sitting.

"Helmet?" So much for surprises being fun. "Where are we going?" No answer. "Tommy?" Alyssa tried to change tactics.

"Not a chance." He laughed over his shoulder from the driver's seat. "She'd kill me."

"He's right." Beth sang happily. Alyssa slouched in the back seat and pouted lightheartedly. How bad could it be?

It was bad!

Chapter Eighteen

"Not happening guys!" Alyssa was being lightly restrained by her friends. The three of them were standing on the middle of a railroad bridge over the Moshannon River. A tall man with a salt and pepper hippie beard was explaining bungee jumping safety rules to them and the ten other crazy people standing up there with them. Several members of the *Adventure Happens* staff were checking (for what Alyssa prayed was at least the tenth time) the bungee jumping equipment. It did not look safe.

"It's going to be fine." Tommy whispered. "My dad took me when I had my birthday. I've been 3 times since. They are a top notch company. Totally safe."

"Then why did I have to sign a *WAIVER?*"

"I told you she wouldn't do it." Tommy whispered at Beth.

"She's doing it." Beth's whisper was doing that annoying singing thing Beth favored so much.

"If I'm doing this then can you two shut up so I know how *not to die!*" Alyssa's whisper turned the entire crowd toward her. It was a possibility that Alyssa wasn't whispering anymore.

Salt and pepper guy cleared his throat. "Okay guys! It's a full docket today, and we're burning daylight!

Crazy number one was being strapped to crazy instructor number one. All new jumpers had to go down double with an instructor. Alyssa didn't see how adding weight to the rope thing was supposed to make her feel safer. She considered making a run for it—Beth caught her after half a step.

"It's *my* birthday! Shouldn't I get to pick how we celebrate? Whatever happened to cake and ice cream?"

"You're gonna love it. The adrenaline is a total rush!" Tommy looked so excited. He was definitely deranged. "I'm gonna go ahead of you. Just watch me."

"You need to do this Alyssa! Trust me." Beth turned her back around.

"How could scaring the crap out of myself possibly be very beneficial?" Her whisper had become a whine. Crazy number three was bouncing away at the end of that rope.

"Well, you have a tendency to avoid scary things. I figure if you can jump off a bridge—calling Brent will be cake."

"Beth! Can you just leave that alone! I'm not celebrating my birthday by throwing myself off a bridge!"

"Happy birthday."

They both turned to find one of the crazy instructors. He was probably a couple years older than them, but not old enough to have been doing this very long. "You're my instructor?" Alyssa was getting more doubtful by the minute.

"You don't look pleased." He smiled at her and handed over the harness she needed to wear. "That's too bad. I'm Chris." He pointed to where his name was stenciled onto his shirt.

"Alyssa." She shook his hand. "No offense, but could I maybe wait for someone...umm...more experienced?"

"Don't worry. I haven't dropped anybody yet." He checked the buckles on her harness to be sure they were tight enough. "And someone like you—I'll be holding on real tight." He grinned up at her. Alyssa ignored his attempts to put her at ease.

It was Tommy's turn and Beth ran to the railing to watch. Alyssa preferred not to, so she closed her eyes.

"You don't want to watch with your friend?" The instructor asked.

"At the moment I'm not sure either of them are my friends." Alyssa groused. This brought a confused look from Chris. "I am kind of here under duress." She continued. "It's their birthday gift to me."

"Ahh." He nodded. "And you don't want to do it?"

"Not really." Alyssa decided she could be honest with Beth out earshot. "Actually, I do want to. I'm just really, really scared."

"If it helps—I don't mind if you scream on the way down. Most girls do."

"I do not *scream*." Alyssa's competitive pride came out to play.

"My turn!" Beth was excited! She was absolutely deranged. "You aren't going to chicken out on me if I go first are you?" She was giving Alyssa a suspicious look even as her instructor connected their harnesses.

"No. I'm right behind you. Go on—go check on your man." Alyssa tried to sound light and convincing. But she wasn't really certain that when her turn came she'd be able to do it.

"So that's how it is? I was wondering how to ask. Figured one of you had to be attached to him." Chris was talking as he walked her over to the staging area so salt and pepper guy could check them over.

"Beth and Tommy? Yup they're pretty much attached at the hip, sorry." Alyssa was trying not to hear Beth's screams over the side of the bridge. Salt and pepper guy was counting backwards.

"I didn't say I was disappointed in which one." He winked at her as he wrapped his arms tightly around her torso. Before she even realized they'd been moved and hooked up to the rope, she heard the word "go!" And *go* they did—right over the edge.

It was amazing! *Rush* did not even begin to describe it. It felt like flying. Her only complaint was that it was too short. She hadn't even screamed.

"That was incredible!" Alyssa was rushing over to where Beth and Tommy were waiting for her.

"And you didn't even scream." Chris piped up from behind her. She hadn't realized he was still following her after they disentangled themselves.

"I told you! Oh, man! Amazing." She was kind of speechless. So her words seemed detached and unintelligent. She didn't care.

Chris was chuckling at her, and holding something out in his hand. "I'd love to take you jumping again. Take my card. We'll get you into the next tour."

"Thanks. Don't these things fill up quick?"

"I'll squeeze you in." He pressed the card into her palm. "Happy birthday again, Alyssa. Nice to meet you both. Have a safe drive." Chris winked one more time at her and jogged away.

"I bet they book a lot of sales that way." Alyssa was saying. "Get you addicted, and then hand out business cards."

"Yeah, that's what he's after. Sales." Tommy was shaking his head and laughing. "Poor guy. And girls think *we're* clueless."

Alyssa thought about that in the car on the ride home. Chris had definitely been flirting with her. At the time she assumed it was his way of putting her at ease, but maybe it had been genuine. Not that it mattered. She wasn't in any more of a dating place now than she had been at the Billy Joel concert.

"When can we go again?" She asked her friends. And they both laughed. What a great way to celebrate her birthday.

Tommy took them to dinner on the drive home, and he even took the liberty of ordering cake and ice cream for dessert. Wisely, he didn't expect the waitresses to sing to her, but he did hum a few bars of happy birthday while they were eating. Beth really was so lucky. Not that Alyssa was jealous, but she did have a new found appreciation for *good guys*. And she was happy her friend had found one.

In school the next Monday Alyssa was having a hard time concentrating. It was a lucky thing for her that she'd been working ahead in most of her classes lately and her grades could afford for her to take an *airhead* day. In calculus the teacher had to call on her three times before Alyssa answered. She'd been wondering why Brent hadn't said anything about his trips to Stoneybrook. Certainly there had been plenty of opportunities during the *time out*. Not that she'd been very keen to discuss Pop at that time.

In her English class she was grateful to be watching a movie she couldn't focus on, because it gave her ample time to reflect on the fact that Brent knew instinctively not to push her into talking about Pop.

At the time she may not have realized it, but half a day talking about Montreal?—that was clearly a diversionary tactic.

Not that all this soul searching reflection was particularly helpful. Mostly it was just confusing herself more. Her weekend had been fine. The Ladybugs won again, and her parents had a small belated party for her on Saturday evening. On Sunday she went to the mall. The one downside to bungee jumping had been that she couldn't find her phone afterwards. Probably it was at the bottom of the Moshannon right now. The upside to losing her phone? Her parents offered to buy her the newest model smart phone as a birthday gift. Of course it had to be ordered and she wouldn't be able to pick it up until next week, but she didn't get that many phone calls these days anyhow. Now it was Monday—here she was without the hecticness of the weekend to distract her, and without that hecticness she had no means with which to drive thoughts of Brent from her mind.

"What's with the return of Zombie Alyssa?" Beth whispered behind her chemistry book.

"I'm not a zombie! I'm just thoughtful today, that's all."

"Still haven't called Brent huh? I told you, you need to stop avoiding things just because they are scary! Look at last weekend. You almost missed out on that jump."

Why did Beth suddenly seem to think she was Yoda? "There isn't much point Beth. He stopped calling me you know. He told me he wasn't in love with me, and then we had this *break*. And now...I don't know, but he didn't even call me on my birthday. That has to mean something right?"

"I don't know about any of that Alyssa. But the guy's crazy about you. You should have seen him that day he went after Pete. Boys don't get that kind of scary about someone they have lukewarm feelings about." Class was over, and they were headed into the hall now. Thankfully the din of shuffling teenagers covered Alyssa's reaction.

"What! When did he go after Pete?"

"Duh, Alyssa. After the party. We talked about this remember? I told you how he was scum and deserved what he got? Didn't you see how bad it was even after you were *sick* for two days?"

"I thought you meant Tommy kicking him in the ribs. You think Brent did that to him?"

Beth pulled Alyssa into the ladies room. "Okay. You really didn't know?"

Alyssa was in shock. All she could do was shake her head from left to right.

"On Sunday when you wouldn't talk to him he called me. So I told him what happened. Or what I was pretty sure happened from the looks of things. I was at Tommy's house at the time. Brent showed up about five minutes after he hung up the phone."

"He came over to tell you he punched Pete?"

"No. He came to get Tommy. Tommy answered the door and they just stared at each other like they were having some kind of man-telepathy conversation. And then Tommy nodded, and said *let's go*. And off they went. Without one word to me. You should have seen it. It would have been sexy if it was on TV or something, but in real life it was kind of scary."

"So Tommy and Brent, like, beat Pete up?"

Beth nodded.

"Wow. No wonder he's given up hassling me. And here I thought it was my tough guy talk." The bell rang. Now they were both going to be late.

Chapter Nineteen

Alyssa didn't get another chance to see Beth for the rest of that day. And she really wanted to finish their conversation. Too much self reflection was driving her in a mental circle. What was the point of having a girlfriend if she couldn't indulge in some girl-talk? Cheer practice was right after school that day, so Alyssa found a spot to work on her calculus homework while she waited for practice to end.

"Want some company?" Alyssa looked up to find Tommy setting his back pack next to hers.

"Sure, umm.... Are you waiting for Beth?"

"Yeah, why?"

"Oh. I was just hoping we would get a chance to finish a conversation we were having earlier."

Tommy nodded. "Not the kind of thing you can talk about in front of *lil ole me*—huh?"

"Nope, no offense though."

Tommy was opening his own calculus book. "None taken, I have a strict policy against delving into the mysteries of a woman's mind."

He was so easy to get along with. A lot like Brent in that way. Alyssa knew how lucky she was to have Beth and Tommy's friendship—especially now that she'd lost Brent's. "Tommy?"

He looked up from his homework.

"I just wanted to thank you. Beth told me about...well about the whole thing with Pete. So, thanks for...defending me I guess. I should have thanked you before. For getting me home safe and all. I was just too embarrassed about the whole thing."

He looked uncomfortable. Maybe she shouldn't have said anything. But she didn't want him to think she was taking him for granted. She learned from her mistakes.

"I didn't do anything to Pete, Alyssa. I would have! He is such an asshole. But that day—it was all Brent."

"Oh. Beth said you were there."

"I was there all right. But we didn't gang up on him. He probably deserved it, but we didn't. That isn't why Brent needed me."

Alyssa had the distinct impression that she was missing something obvious. Clearly Tommy could tell that she wasn't catching on.

"I wasn't there to help him; I was there to stop him. You should have seen him. I'm pretty sure he could have ended up killing Pete if he went alone." Tommy went back to his homework.

Apparently this should have been clear to her. Boys were so dumb! This was why she needed to talk to Beth. Beth would help her understand, because that sounded an awful lot like someone who cared about her. This was strange, considering Brent had barely spoken to her since that weekend. Of course she could have called him back...

"How'd you get that?" He seemed to be studying her practically finished work sheet.

Alyssa showed Tommy how she'd gotten to her answer and helped him correct what he'd already done. "Geez—where have you been all semester?" Tommy joked when they'd finished their homework. "I haven't finished a math assignment this quickly all year. I didn't know you were so smart."

"I'm not." She replied a little embarrassed. "It's just math, everything else Brent—or somebody usually has to help me with. I'm not good at much."

Tommy seemed to be considering this. "I don't know—you're good at this." He waved his worksheet at her. "And you were very good at explaining it. Plus you're great with those softball kids. I bet you'd make a good teacher or something." He went back to packing up his back pack.

Alyssa just stared at him. A teacher. Huh. There was an idea. Automatically she wondered what Brent would think. They'd been friends for 17 years—it was a hard habit to break. Probably he would be all for it. After all, he had said that she was smart. Of course that was before the weirdness, back when they were still friends.

"Practice must be out." Tommy was standing up. Alyssa looked over and saw Jenn Pastings skipping out of the gym's double doors and into a hug with a boy she hadn't noticed waiting there before. He was wearing a familiar maroon blazer.

"Who's that guy?" She asked Tommy.

"I forget his name. Jenn only ever refers to him as her *Hillfield man*."

Alyssa was quite sure she was going to hyperventilate. "That's Jenn's Hillfield boyfriend!"

"Yeah, why? Do you know him?" Tommy was completely ignorant of how insanely important this was.

"No, I don't know him. I know Brent. I thought Brent was her stupid Hillfield man."

Tommy was looking at her like she was speaking Chinese. "Brent and Jenn? That's the dumbest thing I ever heard." He looked away again.

"Were they ever dating?"

"Didn't we just discuss on my policy against getting involved in girly talk?" Probably he was able to tell from Alyssa's face that she wasn't willing to let this go. With the air of a martyr he continued. "As far as I know Brent would never go near her. He's not the kind of guy to take out one girl when he's hung up on another. Although I doubt he'd be interested in any case, seeing as how she's such a bitch. And that's all the girly talk my masculinity can take. You are just going to have to wait for Beth." He sighed. "For real though? You should call him." And he picked up his bag and walked away.

Alyssa didn't wait for Beth. She still needed to have that girl talk, but not now. Of course Brent wasn't seeing Jenn! How could she have been so stupid? Maybe instead of going home she would go see Brent. It would be way uncomfortable, sure, but what was the alternative? Alyssa was just plain tired of avoiding him.

It took her 20 minutes to work up the courage to knock on his door. Ms. Carter answered. "Alyssa! How nice to see you." Her face lit up like a Christmas tree. Maybe Brent hadn't informed her of the recent state of affairs.

"You too, Ms. Carter. Is Brent here? I kinda need to talk to him."

She looked a little confused. "No, dear. He's staying late at school again. There's a lot left to do." Apparently there was something going on at school that Alyssa was supposed to know about. If they were still friends she probably would have.

"Of course. I'll catch him some other time." Very dejectedly Alyssa walked back over to her own house. It was getting late. She should probably start dinner.

As if the universe wanted to add insult to injury, Alyssa paused at her dining room table where right on top of the mail pile she found a big fat manila envelope addressed to her. Return address: Penn State. Filling out her application with Brent felt like a million moments ago. She should be rushing next door right now so they could open them together.

Alyssa revisited her plan of hyperventilation. Fat envelope was good right? Could they have possibly gotten a hold of her Shakespeare paper? Nerves overwhelmed her. That was a surprise. Alyssa had been quite sure she didn't care if she got in, and just as sure that she would turn them down if she did by some miracle get in. What sorts of classes did a teaching degree require?

Alyssa slipped one fingernail beneath the envelope's flap. Just a small tug of her hand and she would know. But she wasn't sure anymore which outcome to hope for. Brent was obviously getting in. Nobody did scholastics like Brent. Alyssa definitely couldn't be on the same campus with him every day. Or in the same classes? No. She wasn't going to be able to handle that. It was too late to apply to anywhere else. Maybe she could put in a semester at the community college and transfer somewhere in the spring? All this planning would be contingent on what she found inside the envelope. Alyssa put it down. She would open it later.

On Friday Beth and Tommy were passionately discussing Gettysburg University vs. Elizabethtown. They'd both been accepted to both schools.

"Have you heard from Penn State yet?" Beth made an effort to include Alyssa.

"Umm, no not really." The envelope was still laughing at her from the top of her dresser. However she had dug out all the old literature she and Brent had sent away for last summer. Penn State had a very good teaching program. So why didn't she just tell Beth the envelope was here, and waiting to be opened? Because, Beth didn't need any more ammunition for her scaredy-cat theory.

Beth misinterpreted Alyssa's dull tone. "We're sorry. Let's talk about something else. What should we do this weekend?"

"There's a movie out I want to see." Tommy piped up too quickly.

"Oh no. Not that street racing movie! I told you I didn't want to see that." Beth replied immediately. "There is an art show at the community center. I wanted go to that."

Tommy looked as if he might be ill if he were forced to attend the art show. "Alyssa will go with you, won't you Alyssa? And I can get some of the guys together for movie."

"Sure, I'll go to the art show." Alyssa was glad to have something to do.

"So what kind of art are we talking about?" Alyssa was asking as she and Beth waited in line outside the community center.

"The ad just said *local talent and various mediums*." Beth answered. "But I thought it looked pretty cool. Is that statue a real person?"

She was pointing to a pedestal where a girl in a long metallic toga style dress was posed. She was covered from head to toe in a metallic paint that matched her dress perfectly. If Alyssa didn't know the community center didn't have statues she would have thought the girl was one. How was standing still an art? Beth however seemed impressed.

Inside the different rooms of the community center had been transformed into galleries. A lot of the exhibits had silent auction papers attached. Some even had sold stickers. Alyssa was impressed and sometimes surprised when she saw the sold stickers. The galleries all seemed to be arranged by type of art. Some held paintings and drawings other's had sculptures. One windowed hallway was displaying a pretty collection of crystal sculptures that threw rainbows onto the opposite wall.

The first gallery they entered had what Alyssa could only assume was *modern art*. What would someone want with sculptures of oversized eating utensils? Even Beth was surprised at that one. Another display was a TV that seemed to be rigged to a motion sensor. As soon as they approached it flickered on and displayed a video a girl climbing in and out of different sized packing boxes. Actually they watched that several times. She didn't get, but it was strangely addictive.

The next room was more enjoyable. The walls were filled with more easily recognized drawings and paintings. Alyssa even jotted down her name and a bid for a particularly pretty snowscape. It was doubtful that she'd win, but the scene sort of reminded her of the landscape photos Brent was so fond of. Maybe if she won, and if she got up the nerve to talk to him again, and if he had any interest in being her friend...well maybe he might like this as a graduation gift or something.

For the most part the galleries were comfortably filled and people were free to mill around from display to display as they pleased. The photography room was crowded. Not that Alyssa blamed anyone. She was partial to photography herself. Beth and Alyssa squeezed past the crowd to check out the pieces hanging on the far wall. Most of the crowd seemed to be concentrating on one exhibit.

"is that her?"

"there she is."

"look over there."

The crowd all seemed to be muttering at once. Beth and Alyssa turned, around to see what was going on, only to find several heads turned in their direction.

"Excuse me miss? Are you the girl from the *heart* photos?" An older woman was talking to her.

Alyssa moved past her without answering. Later on she would feel badly for having ignored her, but now she had to see. Even as she made her way through the crowd though, she knew. By the time the first panel of the exhibit was visible to her she wasn't surprised to see her own face staring down from the large black and white print.

To the left of the exhibit Alyssa could now see a small poster board on a stand. *Brent Carter: Local featured artist.* It said beneath a photo of her best friend. Ex-best friend. It went on to explain Brent was a senior in high school and that one of his teachers had submitted this collection on his behalf. Blah blah blah.

Looking to her right, Alyssa noticed the photos were all hung on large felt covered panels of an accordion style stand; each one angled slightly like the open pages of a book. Above the set up was large banner reading *A Heart in Motion* in an elegant script font. The first photo showed her emptying bottles and trash into the garbage cans at the pond. She wasn't looking at the camera—instead her intent expression was focused on her task.

The next was from the home coming parade. Alyssa's face was shown in profile as she applied glitter to the little girl in a cheer leader costume. This one was vibrant with color. The little girl's happiness was as clear as day. How did he do that? It seemed that every emotion jumped off the wall at her. Somehow Brent was able to capture moments rather than images.

Another panel was hung with several smaller prints—all from the hospital carnival. A montage of children's painted faces, each with her quietly standing in the background. Beneath the frame, where all the pieces of art had yellow silent auction sheets, was a green tag that said *Not For Sale.* Glancing up and down she could tell that each of these photos had green tags. All around her the crowd was making room for her. Either they recognized her face, and therefore her superior claim to being there. Or, and later on Alyssa would think this more likely, they could tell that if they didn't move—she would just have run them right over. At that moment Alyssa was alone in the room with those photos.

There more than a dozen panels. One showed her adjusting Mr. Petry's tie for a date with Sophia Bunch. There was even one of her and Pop. One arm was wrapped around his neck as she pressed a light kiss to his cheek. She remembered him taking this photo. It was about half a second after Pop had extracted that ridiculous promise to take care of Alyssa from Brent.

"Alyssa? Are you okay? Alyssa?" Beth's voice shook her back to reality. Beth was standing to the right of her, and in front of the final panel.

"Yeah, I'm good. I just wish I'd known, you know?"

Beth nodded. "They're beautiful. Not that you aren't always beautiful—but these are something else."

Alyssa knew exactly what she meant. There was a quality about the girl in these photos that Alyssa almost didn't recognize. Certainly seeing this exhibit was a long way from looking at her reflection. This sure wasn't what she saw in the mirror before she left for school in the mornings. Moving to stand behind Beth Alyssa took in the final photo. This was one she didn't remember being taken. Alyssa was half facing away from the camera and her head was turned, smiling over her shoulder. Her moss colored dress betrayed the setting. That was *the* night. The night everything started to fall apart. In the picture only Alyssa was clear—the background was digitally blurred. The effect implying that Alyssa and her smile was the only thing worth seeing.

She looked beautiful, and it wasn't her dress, or her hair and makeup. It was that extra quality she'd been trying to put her finger on. Here it was much more pronounced. Here she was able to identify it. Alyssa stumbled backwards two steps. Beth caught her.

"What's the matter?" She sounded concerned.

"That sonafabitch!"

"Alyssa?" Beth was—understandably—panicking. "Okay, let's get you out of here." She had to half drag Alyssa out of the room. All the while Alyssa was muttering unintelligibly but profanely under her breath.

Chapter Twenty

Beth didn't get any real information out of her the entire drive home. When Alyssa had a mental breakdown—she really did it right. Finally Beth pulled in front of Alyssa's driveway.

"Want me to come in awhile?" Beth sounded hopeful and hesitant at the same time. Not that Alyssa blamed her. Mental breakdown, remember?

"Nope. Thanks for the ride, I had fun." Breakdown or no, Alyssa still had manners.

"Okay, well call me later, if you want to."

Alyssa climbed out of the car and waved to Beth as she drove off. When the car was out of sight she turned on her heel and marched straight over the Carter's house.

Inside the familiar house was full of people. Mostly grownups that looked over dressed for a Saturday afternoon. Alyssa barely noticed them. She stormed down the hallway pausing only for a moment at the entrance to the family room—he wasn't in there. In the kitchen she exchanged polite words with a girl she was reasonable certain she'd met before. Brent's cousin, maybe? Whatever, she said she remembered seeing him outside and that was all Alyssa really cared about.

Outside round tables with long white table clothes were set up all over the backyard under different tents. The big kind that you rent for parties—which Alyssa realized this must be. At the far end of the yard Alyssa could see a band was setting up, and some sort of portable dance floor was in front of them. In a corner by the fence Alyssa spied Brent standing at a small bar. She was too angry with him to notice how incredible he looked. Suits were very kind to him. Alyssa didn't stop to think about what she was going to say. Surely if she stopped to think of anything at all she would scare herself right over that fence and into the safety of her own back yard.

"Alyssa!" Brent turned around just as she reached him. Confusion and maybe a little bit of hope filled his eyes. "What are you doin…"

"You lied to me!" Alyssa interrupted him.

"What! No…"

"You are a liar and I…" Alyssa finished her sentence into the palm of Brent's hand. People were staring, she realized.

"Come on." He closed one hand around her elbow and dragged her into the house and up the stairs. More people stared.

Inside his bedroom Alyssa lost the nerve she'd been fostering since the community center. At one time this was a safe place for her, but now the room was filled with memories of her last visit. Alyssa stood nervously by Brent's desk. That was as far away from his bed as she could manage. Brent turned the lock on the door knob and turned to face her.

They stared at each other.

"Who died?" Alyssa finally managed.

"What?"

"Umm…all those people…I thought maybe a wake?" Alyssa fidgeted.

"Complete with a three piece band? It's my Aunt Carol's wedding." Alyssa's eyes went wide at his explanation. "She didn't want a big deal since it's her second—mom said she could do it here."

"I didn't know she was engaged. I probably shouldn't have interrupted." Alyssa moved towards the door.

Brent was quicker. "Oh, no. Now that you're here you aren't leaving." He was leaning against the door. He looked as panicked as she felt.

Another beat or two passed silently. "I've never lied to you Alyssa." His words came out slowly in a forced calm voice.

"You did. Before—when we were still friends…"

"Still friends?" Brent's face fell. "Aren't we friends now? What happened to taking a break?"

"A break! You haven't called at all. It's been months."

"I called! I called, and I came to your house. Alyssa, you wouldn't let me through the front door. You locked the window!" Brent shoved one hand through his hair. "You can't have any idea what that was like for me. When the window was locked—it was awful, Lyssa. So I figured I'd give you some time, but you never called. And that day before your softball game? Running off on me the way you did? It was worse that the damn window."

"I was late!" Alyssa protested.

"You were early. Really early!"

How did he know that? "How do you know that?"

Brent shifted around where he was standing. "Beth told me. I'm afraid I've been making a nuisance of myself with her and Tommy. I knew when the game was Lyssa. I was there."

"You were at the first softball game?"

"I come to all your games. I just sit on the other team's bleachers. I wasn't sure you'd want me there. You are amazing with those kids."

Alyssa nodded. He came to every game. Last fall he'd told her he would be at every game if she was playing a sport. She wasn't playing, but she supposed this counted.

"Lyssa? When did I lie to you?" Brent took a small step towards her, but then his eyes darted back to the door. As though he was afraid she might get by him, Brent retreated to continue blocking the exit.

"I went to the community center with Beth today. I saw your exhibit."

"Is that what this is about? I told you I was taking those photos! You agreed! You even signed the release form."

Alyssa did remember him making her fill out some paperwork releasing any rights to the photos.

"I'm not mad about the photos. They're great by the way—you were by far the most popular artist."

"Thanks." His voice was impatient. He raised his eyebrows at her.

"At first I couldn't figure it out—why they were so good. I mean you know I think you're a great photographer, but these…"

"Lyssa!"

"Right—well the thing is. You said you weren't in love with me. I asked you. Right here in this room, and you said no. You laughed at me and sent me away. Those photos…well it would seem you do have some feelings for me." Alyssa muttered the last part, now she was feeling pretty stupid.

Brent was struggling against the smile at the corner of his mouth. "I never said I didn't have feelings for you, Lyssa. I believe I said I hadn't been pining for you. Which is true, was true. And I wasn't laughing at you. I was embarrassed. I thought, well I thought it was mutual—and then you apologized for leading me on! I was embarrassed and disappointed."

Alyssa was just staring at him. So he started talking again. "After Christmas, when Pop died—I thought maybe I was wrong. Maybe your feelings had changed too. I waited weeks for you to call." Brent seemed to have run out of things to say, or maybe he was just out of breath.

"You punched Pete." Alyssa changed tactics.

"When Beth told me…" Brent's hands curled into fists. "I wanted to kill him, Lyssa. If I had been with you…"

"It's not your fault. Nothing happened. I was drunk." Alyssa whispered.

"About that. I understand why you were mad. But I didn't know, I mean…" He scrubbed a hand over his face. "When I woke up, and you were in my bed? I thought you were trying to tell me something. I didn't know you were drunk. I get that you were mad—I took advantage. Unintentionally! But I did."

"I wasn't mad. I was just embarrassed." Alyssa mumbled. "You might have girls in your bed all the time, but I wasn't sure…I mean I'm sure it was great, but…" She trailed off.

"Lyssa?" Brent abandoned his post at the door, and came to stand in front of her. Not touching her, but close enough for the air to buzz with implied intimacy. "Lyssa, what do you think happened?

Alyssa couldn't believe he was going to make her say it. "I woke up in your bed, and in your shirt."

"Oh Lyssa! No, wonder you hated me." Brent pulled her into a tight hug. Wrapping his big arms around her shoulders he continued to speak softly into her ear. "You must have thought I was just like Pete. How could you? Don't you know me any better than that?"

"Didn't we?"

"No! I did think…I mean I was still half asleep at first, but when I realized you'd been drinking, and your arm! Lyssa I couldn't believe how bad it was." He pulled out of their embrace enough to examine her now healed arm. His big hand brushed lightly over the areas that had been bruised. "When I came back with the ice pack you'd umm…stripped down to your underwear and you were almost asleep. It was all I could do to get a shirt on you before you were out."

"We didn't sleep together?" Alyssa was a little behind.

"No. But, but I wanted to Lyssa. It was very…difficult…to fall back asleep that night. When I woke up and you were gone—I thought it would kill me. And when you wouldn't even talk to me—I could only take so much rejection Lyssa."

"I wasn't rejecting you! I just…" Alyssa blew a strand of hair out of her face. "Well apparently I have a tendency to avoid things that are scary." She finished.

If Brent found anything amiss with that explanation he wisely kept his piece about it. "I scare you?" A big slow smile lit up his face.

"Is that good? Do you want to be scary?" Alyssa thought he might be a little insane. But at least being here and talking to him was getting easier. He was still Brent.

"I want to be something! Lyssa if I scare you at all, then that gives me some hope. I miss you so much."

"I miss you too. All the time." Alyssa took a deep breath. "Just so I'm clear…are you saying that you do have feelings for me?"

"It was that day at the hospital. Who's the redheaded girl? She was dressed like a ladybug."

"You have feelings for Brittany? She's in the tenth grade!"

Brent was laughing at her. "No. I don't. But Brittany spent most of that afternoon sobbing over one kid or another. Hugging them and talking about how brave they were. She was a total downer."

"Are you trying to change the subject?"

"No. Would you just listen?" Brent was grinning at her. "You never cried or shied away. That little boy? The one that wanted the spider web on his head? You were his hero. I was blown away by you that day. You were incredible. That's when I knew...that I was completely, totally, and irrevocably in love with you."

"Oh." Alyssa didn't have enough breath to manage more than that one word.

"If I kiss you, are you going to run screaming out the window?" Brent was an inch away from her face.

"No. I think if were to you kiss me, I might be inclined to stay—quite a while." Alyssa teased.

Nothing happened. They stood there close enough to taste each other, but Brent never moved.

"Did you change your mind?" Alyssa finally pulled away from him.

"I think I am very nervous." Brent chuckled and lowered himself into his desk chair pulling Alyssa down into his lap.

"And here I thought you were mister experience." Alyssa chuckled too. It was such a relief to be able to tease him again.

"Twice."

"What?" Alyssa wasn't sure if he wasn't making sense, or if being this close to him was addling her brain.

"You seem to think that I *have girls in my bed all the time*. It is hardly a part of my daily routine. Once over the summer—I met a girl when I went to the beach with my dad. And then last September Melissa's parents went out of town for the weekend."

"Well twice is still more than me—how come you wouldn't tell me when I asked before, and now you're mister details?"

"Because Lyssa...there are some things I don't think you should share with your friends, but that my girlfriend deserves to know."

"And now I'm your girlfriend?"

"Is that weird?" Brent pulled her even more tightly to him.

"Not a bit, now about that kiss..." Alyssa fluttered light kisses over his cheek closer and closer to his mouth.

"I hate that you have bad memories of our first kiss. I think this one needs to be very very good to make up for it." Turning his head Brent closed the remaining distance.

It was the single most amazing kiss in Alyssa's memory. His mouth slanted against hers, his tongue softly explored the contours of her mouth. She wanted to stay frozen in that moment forever. Someone knocked on the door.

"Brent? Carol and Tim are leaving."

"Tell them bye for me, mom." Brent reached for Alyssa again. But she pulled away, suddenly nervous. Brent thought that was funny.

"Honey, is Alyssa in there with you?" Ms. Carter sounded worried.

"Yes, mom. Lyssa came over to have a talk." He was full on grinning now. Alyssa wanted to crawl under the purple stained rug.

"Okay then. I'll give your best to Aunt Carol." She actually sounded relieved! Not that she'd ever minded Alyssa being in her son's room before, but they'd never locked the door before either.

"Do you think she knows?" Alyssa whispered.

"Definitely." Brent kissed her again. "But I'm sure she prefers this to the alternative. I haven't been very easy to live with lately. So...how was it Chere? Good enough to make up for the first time?"

"I don't know. Maybe we should try it again."

And then they didn't have much else to talk about.

Epilogue

"Six hundred twelve!"

Alyssa turned away from the closet to see Brent filling the door frame. "Six hundred twelve what?" She rushed over to give him a kiss.

"Steps from my dorm room to yours." Brent was grinning at her. "And since I have two roommates and you only have one...we'll be spending a lot of our time here." Brent swept her up and they landed together on her tiny twin bed. The aforementioned roommate was at the campus bookstore. "I have something for you." Brent pulled a small black ring box from his pocket.

Alyssa lost her ability to breathe. Her panic must have shown on her face, because Brent rolled his eyes at her. This didn't bother her nearly as much these days.

"Don't have a heart attack Chere." He lifted the lid to reveal a ring with two silver hands clasping a heart. "I bought it last year actually. I meant you to have it for Christmas but..." He let the sentence trail off. They'd rehashed those lost months enough over the summer. "Worn this way it is a friendship ring." He lifted it from its box. "and this way" he turned the ring so the heart pointed inward "means you belong to someone. You belong to me."

"I love it." Alyssa let him slip the ring onto her finger. "I bought you a tripod. Pretty lame huh?"

"No way! Is it here?"

"Nah, it's at home. You can have it next weekend."

Brent pulled her close to him. "That's cool. I'm not thinking about cameras right now anyway." When he'd finished kissing her senseless he had another question for her. "Are going to react that way when it's the real thing?"

"What?" He was confusing her.

"The next time I give you a ring box, Lyssa. I'd like to know if you are going to have another deer in the headlights moment."

"You mean if we...I thought it was a..."

"Duh, Lyssa. I mean *when* I propose. Don't get me wrong—we should probably get through college first. But I think that's where this is headed. I've been in love with you forever. It just took me 18 years to notice."

"I love you too. I promise—no deer in the headlights." Alyssa kissed him again.

"When's your roommate coming back?" Brent wanted to know.

"She's going to dinner after the bookstore." Alyssa whispered.

Keep reading for a sneak peak at

TJ Dell's new series…

Whispers in the Woods

Chapter One

The convenience store was closed. I must have yanked on that locked door four times before my brain finally accepted that *Jack's* was closed for the evening. Nothing in Chicago closes at ten o'clock. As if I really needed one more reason miss home. I'd asked Gram where the nearest 7-Eleven was—that conversation took fifteen minutes and innumerable grunts before I understood that the town of Benair Falls didn't boast a brand-name convenience store. *Everyone goes to Jack's if they need a little something.* Apparently I should have pushed Gram a little harder if I wanted her to volunteer the information that the store had already closed before I'd even left the house. The two mile bike ride back to my grandmother's home seemed much longer without the promise of a Slurpee at the end of the trip.

My friends laughed at me back home when I didn't bother taking the driving test with the rest of them after our classroom driver's ed course. Boy was I regretting that decision now. Not that I'm too out of shape for a two mile bike ride. Actually I am in very good shape—but I'd been riding a rusty thirty year old Huffy I'd found in Gram's shed the month before. Not my favorite choice for exercise.

My last day in Chicago was September 15th – a Thursday. My best friend Claire's mom made pancakes from scratch that morning. Mom had always been more of a run-to-the-corner-for-bagels kind of a breakfast person. But that morning I woke up in Claire's apartment and I ate pancakes, because that was where I'd been staying since the funeral.

Mom and Dad both died in the car accident. I have a scar on my neck and collar bone. How crazy is that? A scar. Gram stayed in a hotel while the arrangements were made. I stayed with Claire.

If you are getting the impression that Gram is a sweet little old lady who spends her days baking cookies and bragging about me to her bridge club then you should probably go back and reread something. Gram doesn't want me. She doesn't want anybody. Mom left here 18 years ago when she met my dad, and I never even met Gram until after they'd died. I, by the way, was sixteen. Sixteen is a lot of years to go without contacting your only grandchild—particularly when she lives in an apartment building only 2 hours away. (That's by car—not Huffy)

Back at Gram's I parked the bike on the front porch, and went upstairs to my bedroom. I use the term *my* loosely. Gram calls it the guest room. There is a full sized bed pushed into a corner under the window to make room for a big ugly antique dresser to squeeze next to the headboard. Against another wall I put up a portable clothes rack. The guest room closet was filled with every dress and pants suit Gram had ever bought. Each sealed up in a plastic garment bag. She never offered to move them.

I wasn't exactly insulted. I'd always known there was a reason we spent thanksgiving at a *Boston Market*. Mom never talked about Gram. I used to think it was about my dad. This would probably have explained some of her hostility towards me too. But it didn't take me long to realize that Gram was an equal opportunity hater. She hated her hair dresser for suggesting a little coloring. She hated the mailman for coming too early in the mornings and getting the neighbor's dog barking. She hated the neighbors for having a dog. You get the point.

I'd been living with Gram for a little more than a month at this point. So her hostility didn't really affect me that much anymore. To be honest it never affected me all that much to begin with. I suppose I was still in a little bit of shock from the accident or whatever. When I got around to noticing her...let's call it unconventional...behavior I was actually a little relieved. Because I didn't really want to be happy in Benair Falls.

10:30 was still a little early for me to go to sleep on a Friday night, but I didn't have anything better to do. So I grabbed my little bathroom bag (Gram didn't have room for my things in the bathroom either) and headed for a shower. I love a hot shower first thing in the morning. I tend to have a difficult time waking up without one. Gram loves hot showers in the mornings too. The house is old and has a small water heater, so I get to shower at night. I do not love going to bed with a wet head.

Not being particularly sleepy, I had ample opportunity to think once I'd climbed into bed and after I'd given up my nightly efforts to find a comfortable portion of the rock hard mattress. Mostly I was thinking about my friend Claire. For me, missing Claire and missing Chicago were strangely comforting. Because it was too hard to miss Mom and Dad. Of course what I mean is that it was too hard to think about missing them. I did miss them very much, but it was easier to think about Claire. Claire and I had lived in the same building since we were kids.

Our moms would take us to the park together, we rode the school bus together, we even had crushes on the smokin' hot teenage boy that worked the welcome desk in the lobby the summer we were 13 together. Claire and I didn't have much in common. I liked school—she liked copying my answers. I liked swimming in the pool—she liked lounging *by* the pool. I was a cheerleader and on the school paper—she had a boyfriend. Those last two are connected, I promise. Claire treated her relationship with Trent like an extra-curricular. The point is that we weren't typical best friends. Actually if it weren't for our geographical circumstances (same building, remember?) we probably wouldn't have been friends. I still missed her.

Even self pity has some limits, and I guess mine was five weeks. This particular night missing Claire didn't hold its usual dark entertainment quality for me. I had exactly one friend in Benair Falls. Anna King. Anna's locker was next to mine at school. So once again my friendship was determined by geography. A less confident girl might wonder if she was even able to make friends based on her own merit. As it happens I was about to make the most amazing friend I would ever know. But I don't want to get ahead of the story.

Anna King said hello to me on my first day of school. I had put my messy hair in a messy head band and worn old worn jeans with black Van Halen t-shirt. I don't actually listen to much Van Halen, but when I was in the tenth grade I went through a 'retro' phase and I'd pillaged my mom's storage unit. At the time I didn't bother too much with *why*. If you've ever lost a parent you understand the frozen numbness that follows you around afterwards. Now that I'd begun to thaw I could have told you I'd dressed that way to make sure everyone steered clear of me. I wasn't ready to be peppy. I didn't want people to ask me about the scar that was still pretty gruesomely visible above the collar of my shirt. Gram didn't think keeping me out of school could possibly be beneficial any longer.

The thing about being the new kid in a small town? You are big news. The outfit didn't work; everyone said hi to me that day anyway. I mostly ignored them. I spent a lot of time perfecting my scowl that first week.

By the next week I was really tired of my *scary* band shirts. So I started fixing my hair, wearing colors, and carrying my essential lip gloss. However, the damage was already done. I'd been branded a loner. Only Anna said hello to me after that. Being a loner wasn't all bad; at least I didn't have to hear a bunch of *I'm sorry about your parents* comments. And I really do like Anna. Anna is the kind of sweetly annoying person that won't let you spend all day wallowing in your own misery. Sweet— because she really is, and annoying—because she's right about the whole wallowing thing. I tried not to be too annoyed though. Since, like I said, she was the only one bothering to talk to me.

Anna just seemed to decide we were friends. She showed up after my last class one day to offer me a ride home and was there the next morning to take me to school. Which I jumped at, because wallowing or no wallowing I hated being the oldest person riding the school bus. I didn't even let it bother me when she asked about *my heritage*. Although I did have to laugh at the way she said it.

It was during our short ride from school to Gram's house. Normally Anna was bubbling with news of her day, or of which cute boy she was in love with.

"You're so pretty, Evie." Anna was concentrating extra hard on the road.

"Thanks, Anna. You're pretty too."

"No, I mean I think your complexion is pretty."

"Oh. Well still, thanks." I hadn't caught on at this point. I was *that* used to people *not* mentioning it.

"I wondered umm, about your heritage. Cause your mom was like me right?" Anna is sweet. You have to remember that. I was actually trying so hard not to laugh at this point I had to hold my breath. Now that I think about it—that was the first time in a month I'd felt any compulsion towards laughter.

"My mom was white. Dad was black." Anna blanched a little. "African American." I corrected myself. She seemed to accept that term more easily.

I knew she wasn't prejudiced. She was Tom Master's English tutor. Tom and Billy are the two other African American students. Apparently she just expected me to be more PC in my terminology.

No one at Benair High looks like me. When I was four a little girl at my Gymboree class asked me why I *looked like chocolate milk*. When my dad found out he had this really long serious talk with me about how god took a *little bit of him and a little bit of mommy mixed it all up and sent them me with my pretty caramel skin*. We also talked about how I would probably meet a lot of people in my life that would treat me differently because of the way I look. And that some of them would even be mean. In reality that was the last time anyone ever brought it up to me until Anna asked. There were a lot of kids from mixed families at my school in Chicago. There were a lot of *kids* at my school in Chicago. In Benair Falls we have one black family. Tom and Billy are twins and they are in the ninth grade.

So when Anna got up the nerve to ask me about it I was more surprised than anything else. Just one more stupid thing to dislike about this stupid town. For the first time in my life I was a minority. Although to be fair no one treated my any differently—at least not until after I was so rude that first week. I've always liked the way I look. My hair takes a little more work in the morning than mom's straight blond tresses ever did.

But I like the way my spiky dark brown curls look better. That chocolate milk analogy from 12 years ago came back to me after the accident. Every day, I look in the mirror and see a little of each of my parents. So yeah, I like the way I look.

The mental examination of my two friendships (In Chicago I had many friends) did the trick. I was finally sleepy enough to close my eyes. It would be a while before I realized this, but that was the last time I would fall asleep as a normal teenage girl. The next day my life was going to change and the ramifications of that change would be life-long.

Chapter Two

I could feel the damp before I opened my eyes. The morning was shrouded in a heavy fog. Up until then we'd been experiencing a nice run of Indian summer. Autumn was here at last.

A few months before weather like this would have seen me curling up back in my bed with a good book. I didn't like the idea of autumn or, even worse, winter keeping me in this gloomy house. So I pulled a sweatshirt over my head, laced up my heavy boots, and headed outside.

If I was going to like something about Benair Falls, and I'm not saying I do. But if I did, it would be the scenery. Dad used to take me hiking all the time. Mom was more the type to spend a Saturday touring a department store. We always had to plan ahead though, because before we could walk we had to drive. In Benair Falls I only have to walk one short block and cross one seldomly used road to reach the park. From the park you could access a number of nice wooded hiking trails. That is where I'd been spending most of my Saturdays and Sundays. You can imagine Gram's relief.

The park was totally deserted. Of course it was 7:00 in the morning, and the fog made things dismal at best. I didn't let it bother me. As a matter of fact the weather matched my mood. Anna had wanted me to join her for a movie that day—she always had something planned on the weekends. I always turned her down. I don't know why. It isn't like I didn't want to have fun—it was just harder than it used to be.

Less than an hour later I was settled on a fallen log munching on a granola bar. My butt was getting wet. Dad would have thought to bring a blanket—something water proof. I was just deciding to make a trip to the sporting goods store in search of wet-weather gear when I saw him.

The trail followed a bend off to the left. He came from the right. I remember thinking it was weird that the fog was getting heavier and more dense. The sun was up by then and it should have gone a long way towards clearing up the weather. There in the woods, everything went still and heavy; I could feel the pressure difference when I tried to breathe in. A moment later I saw him ambling out from between thick trees. I thought I must have zoned out thinking about dad, because surely I would have noticed sooner if someone was traipsing around through the woods in complete disregard for the trails.

He would have been very hard to miss. He was big. Probably 6'4" and really wide too. Not fat wide—even in his heavy sweatshirt I could appreciate the toned muscles propelling him easily through the thick growth.

"Hi, I'm Lucas." Stepping out of the trees and onto the path, he joined me on my wet log without hesitating. As though that was his destination all along.

I know better than this. A strange man approaches you in the woods? Run. I know those are the rules. I should have been halfway back to Gram's before he cleared the tree line. I was completely unable to move. He was even more incredible up close.

It's like I was lost the moment I looked into his dark brown eyes with long lashes that should have been feminine, and yet somehow weren't. I can't say how long I stared into those eyes. Eventually he shifted; lifting one long leg to straddle the log, he turned to face me more fully. The action shook me enough that I was able to take in the rest of him. I thought he might be in his early twenties. His hair was only a shade or two lighter than his eyes and it was long. I couldn't say for sure how long because he wore it in ponytail at the base of his neck, but at least six inches of smooth straight hair hung beneath the elastic band. Still, he was nothing less than pure masculinity. Even his nose was perfect. I am sure this was the first time I'd ever noticed a man's nose, but his was perfectly straight exactly the right shape and—well how do you describe a perfect nose?

"And you are?" He was unperturbed by my long silence. How long must I have been staring?

"My butt is getting wet." That's right. Let it be known that at the most important moment of my life I said *my butt is getting wet.*

To his tremendous credit—he didn't laugh.

"It's the weather. I'm sure things will dry off soon." He leaned closer to me bracing himself with one hand on the log between us.

"I meant to say…. My name is Evie—Evelyn Parker, but Evie for short."

He smiled. A slow wide smile that, if possible, improved his appeal even more. "I'm glad to meet you Evie." The way he said my name—it was like he was tasting the words.

We stared at each other for awhile. I was thinking he was crazy for sitting there with me, but at the same time I was terrified at the idea that he might leave. Where had he come from anyway?

"Where did you come from?"

He looked confused. "I was hiking. Same as you."

"No. I was using the trails."

He screwed up his face for a minute. "There are more trails. Just over there." He gestured into the trees with one open hand.

"Okay." I accepted his lie.

I had explored every inch of those woods and I knew all the trails. There was nothing in the direction he was pointing. I couldn't figure out why he would lie, but I let it go since I was already pretty embarrassed at my lack of social graces. I am not normally the type to get tongue tied by a good looking boy—but he was more than just good looking and more man than boy.

He nodded, still smiling at me. "You look sad."

For almost two months I'd been telling everyone how *fine* I was. I'm not sure why, but I told Lucas the truth. "I am."

"You don't want to talk about it?" I shook my head from side to side. "So, you like hiking?" He didn't press me at all. I was sad that was all there was to it—moving on.

"I do. My dad used to take me. I come here a lot. This log and I have gotten to be good friends." I found my smile. I was enjoying talking with him. "I've only been in town a few weeks."

As I felt more comfortable I was able to notice more than his handsome face. For instance I realized our log-bench was now dry and warm. Above us the sun was shining down easing the heaviness in the air. The humidity didn't dissipate completely but the strange pressure from a few moments before was gone now.

"I know. I would have remembered if we'd met somewhere." His smile became a grin. This ridiculously beautiful man was flirting with me in my sweats and hiking boots. "Do you like it here?"

I told him. I told him about my Gram being less than hospitable and about Anna trying so hard to be my friend. I told him about my parents and that I hadn't felt whole since the accident. That I often felt as though I was seeing my own life through a window; I could see and hear what was going on around me but I wasn't really a part of it all. Lucas was a patient listener. He made the occasional comment, but mostly he just listened. I hadn't spoken so much at one time since before I'd come to Benair Falls. When I ran out of things to say I realized that without my noticing he had slid closer to me and the small of my back was now pressed against his solid thigh, my shoulder nestled into his. His warmth and the kindness shining down from his eyes felt wonderful. I forgot how to breathe again.

"Are you all right?" He eyes crinkled up like he was trying not to laugh at me. I suppose that at that moment I was quite laugh-at-able. I'd just stopped talking and started staring at him. I probably looked like a lunatic.

"Fine." I managed to say after I'd drawn a few ragged breaths. "Umm, that's a lot about me. Can we talk about you?" Like what movie set you escaped from? I couldn't help adding to myself.

"What do you want to know?"

"Are you from around here?" Lame I know, but you wouldn't blame me if you'd seen him up-close. It was extremely difficult to think of anything interesting to say.

"I move around a lot. But I always end up back here—I like it here very much."

"Like with your family? Your parents travel for work or something?"

"Or something." He was clearly still trying not to laugh. If he hadn't been so damn attractive I would have been angry. "Tell me more about school. You attend Benair High?"

"It's the only high school in town."

"Of course. And you're in the twelfth grade?"

"I'm a junior." He looked like he didn't understand. "The eleventh grade." I clarified for him. Understanding filled his face. Where had he gone to school that he didn't know the term 'junior'?

We talked for hours. Sometimes about more heavy topics, such as my parents and my grandmother and sometimes we settled on lighter subjects such as his love of action films. I like a good adrenaline charge as much as the next person, but cars crashing and exploding buildings get old after awhile.

"Well I guess we won't be going to many movies than, will we?" He teased me when I admitted I was more of a sappy love-story-Sandra-Bullock-type fan. My breath caught in my throat at the implication. But he was probably just teasing.

I told him about my Slurpee obsession and consequent disappointment in Benair's lack of 7-elevens. He unabashedly admitted a similar relationship with Krispy Kreme Donuts.

I didn't even notice how much time had passed until my stomach growled. It was really loud.

"You are hungry." He seemed delighted. "Let me take you to lunch."

"Thanks, no. I should get back. My Gram is probably waiting for me."

He had to know I was lying. We'd devoted a lot of the morning to the crappy state of my home life. But he let me get up and leave. It isn't that I wanted to say no, but I had a strange feeling that the magic of the morning would be broken once we left the woods. So I left. I walked away leaving him sitting on my log-bench.

T.J. Dell

<u>More Works by T.J. Dell</u>
Her Best Friend's Brother
Smile For Me
Whispers in the Woods (The Elfkin Series)
A Dog Named Jingle Bells

For more information and for upcoming release dates
find T.J. at <u>Facebook.com/dell.tj</u>

Made in the USA
Las Vegas, NV
07 November 2024

11215224R00085